ROUND THE CABIN TABLE

ROUND THE CABIN TABLE

Yarns of an Old Cruising Man

Maurice Griffiths

Illustrated by the author

These yarns are dedicated to Coppie, my patient wife, who nobly gave up her interests in horses and a career in the WRNS in order to share with me some of the discomforts of pottering about in little yachts.

NOTE: Some of the yarns in this book have appeared in a different form in *Yachting Monthly*, to whose Editor I am greatly obliged for permission to include them in this volume.

By the same author:
The Magic of the Swatchways
The First of the Tide
Dream Ships
Little Ships and Shoal Waters
The Hidden Menace

First published in Great Britain in 1985 by
Conway Maritime Press Ltd
24 Bride Lane
Fleet Street
London EC4Y 8DR

Designed by Tony Garrett
Typesetting and artwork by Sunset Phototype, Barnet
Printed and bound in Great Britain by Oxford University Press

CONTENTS

Illustrations

Introduction

In less than a generation pleasure boating, from wind-surfing and water skiing to deep water cruising and offshore racing, has become the pastime of millions. It is all part of a democratic philosophy to welcome these changes in lifestyle which enable so many to have so much leisure with so much money to enjoy it all together in healthy activities on the water. It is a blessing which in the years before the Hitler War could be indulged in by only a few.

It is perhaps as well, therefore, that the younger boating enthusiasts have become conditioned to expect overcrowding in all worthwhile sports: to be patient when having to queue for nearly everything, and to accept noise – from spluttering out-board motors, clanging halyards on metal masts, loud hailers from the shore, the drone of skiboats, or canned music across the water – as essential to put the *pleasure* in pleasure boating today. With a recorded quarter of a million yachts, sailing dinghies and motor craft in Great Britain today, recreational boating has become one of the leading growth sports.

With this explosion in yachting and all the facilities afforded the boating man and his family, there has come a sea-change in the pattern of weekend cruising as we older yachtsmen used to know it. The premium on berths in any yacht harbour, and the convenience afforded the family of lying alongside a pontoon with all a yacht marina's services at hand, make it unattractive to cast off the mooring lines, stow the fenders inboard, and leave one's berth for a night or two away. A quick out-and-back sail each day has become the norm for most family boats, in case some overnight visiting yacht slides into the vacant berth and is discovered resting like a cuckoo in the nest.

Few yachts drop their anchors away from their base these days, with the result that on many boats the anchor and cable, and the kedge or second anchor with its warp, have become rarely used pieces of equipment. Indeed, the ship's one-time prime item of gear, her anchor, is only to be found aboard many contemporary yachts stowed with its nylon line inside a locker beneath the foredeck. Old Cold Nose has retired from view, like an unwanted poor relative.

Much of the traditional independence of the weekend cruising man has been eroded away in these days of enforced uniformity, and the overnight cruising around the coast that is now carried out frequently takes the form of organised cruises in company. These can be highly successful affairs, and a great boost to the morale of the more timid sailing crew; and the custom of including a beach barbecue and a general get-together of crews with a sing-song brings a thoroughly matey air to the scene, which can be shared by the whole crowd in their bobble caps and yellow wellies.

Yet there are still those – only a small minority now – who long for the peace and the solitude to be found only in such places as in woodlands, or on the moors, high up in the craggy hills, or on board a small boat. Despite the swarms of small craft which every summer weekend will be found milling around the more popular anchorages, clustering together as close as can be to the nearest hard or landing stage, there *are* still good safe anchorages to be found away from the crowds.

For the man or woman who enjoys such solitude there is nothing I know to compare with the feeling of comfort and homeliness of one's own little ship, however plain and humble she may be. When the anchor is down, the riding light hoisted

[Time for the riding light]

on the forestay for the night, and the hatch closed against the cool night air, a small yacht's cabin can become the cosiest place in the word. When the soft light from the gimballed lamp throws its warm glow over the surrounding varnish work, and reflects like liquid gold from its brass surface and the polished rims of the portlights, while in the night outside the tide flows softly past the sides of the hull, and waders call to each other as they feed along the shoreline, this is the time for the crew to relax and savour its quietude.

This is when old logbooks may be turned up, the chart unrolled, and yarns retold of days and nights at sea, of struggles with reef points and wet flogging canvas, of the half-swamped dinghy breaking its painter before the angry following seas and disappearing into the night, of that time no one knew where they were until the yacht's keel stuck the sands with a sickening jarring thud . . . And yet one would also recall days of soft warm breezes, nights calm with stars reflected like diamonds on the water. It is of such days and nights of utter contrast – for no two days are ever exactly alike at sea – that I have written in these pages, in the hope that the reader may share some of the experiences that I have encountered during some sixty years of sailing around our coasts in a variety of small craft.

MAURICE GRIFFITHS
West Mersea
Essex

[Squally day in the Wallet Spitway]

[Edwardian maybe, but warm and
inviting]

– 1 –
What was it like?

Yarns of cruising in small yachts on the East Coast before the Hitler War have so often been met with unbelieving expressions and questions like "what was it *really* like, sailing in those days?" that I have often been asked to recall something of the ordinary weekend yachtsman's activities half a century or more ago.

For one thing, there were far fewer boats afloat, and not so many moorings. Although favourite places close to hards and landing stages such as Burnham anchorage, Brightlingsea Creek, West Mersea, Walton Channel and Pin Mill seemed to be full of moorings, the trots had not yet spread both up and down the channel in long rows as far as the eye could see, and, as yet, no one could imagine the need to install mooring posts or pontoons for doubled-up berthing.

There were then no regulated yacht harbours on the East Coast with the exception of Lowestoft, and the American term 'marina' was not imported until many years later. Indeed, the first artificial harbours for yachts in this country – Cubitt's Basin at Chiswick and the mill pool at Birdham near Chichester – had still to be dug out and filled with boats.

Swinging moorings afloat were the normal thing, while there was usually plenty of room for visiting yachts to anchor above or below the moorings. Yachts used their anchors far more frequently then than now, and most of us cruising types had our favourite spots for letting go Old Cold Nose for the night. Ah, what fun it was to bring up in three fathoms or so in a sheltered reach, with the dew already glistening in the soft rays of the riding light hanging on the forestay, and to listen to the hissing sound of the mud as the tide left it bare while the cries of the sea birds came shrill and haunting across the dark line of the sedge grass. A peaceful evening, a warm cabin and not another boat in sight.

Most of us knew of such anchorages in the Crouch and the Roach or, dropping down on the ebb from Maldon or Heybridge, the sheltered reach below the 'Doubles' with four feet in it at low water, or, with a fresh nor' westerly blowing, a quiet night close in to Osea pier. With east in the wind there was a deserted anchorage under the lee of the land between Colne Point and Brightlingsea Creek, when the latter was full of craft and Pyefleet open to the wind. Even up Colne, just below the entrance to Alresford Creek, was a snug enough anchorage.

In breezy easterly weather Harwich Harbour and the Stour would appear unfriendly for the small boat man, but a favourite anchorage of mine was a cable's length inside the Walton buoy (just above what is now the huge Felixstowe Dock complex), just outside the ship channel and close to the sheltering mud in a fathom and a half. Even today, not many yachts make use of this berth – but it's not suitable with any west in the wind. In days gone by you would find a yacht brought up in quiet weather for the night far away from the more popular anchorages, like Pennyhole Bay under the Naze, along the edge of the Gunfleet sands, or, as I often lay, halfway up the Rays'n channel under the lee of the Dengie Flats. People today often seem hell-bent on motoring for hours so as to get some overcrowded anchorage.

Before we all had cars to get down to our little ships the Day of the Train meant as much to us as it does now to Jimmy Savile. In fact there were many advantages in not being tied to a parked car. Dating back to before World War One negotiations between the Cruising Association and the old Great Eastern Railway had made special weekend tickets available to yachtsmen, allowing one to return from any part of the East Coast, paying only the excess fare when the port of arrival was farther than that of departure.

It was easy therefore to take a fair wind from, say, Fambridge or Burnham round to Walton Naze, Pin Mill, Woodbridge or Aldeburgh, leave the boat there and catch the Sunday evening train home. A week or two later a fair slant would bring a fine sail back to your home waters; and what a wonderful sense of freedom that gave you as you cast off next weekend not knowing where you would be leaving the boat for the following week or so.

There was no problem getting back to London by train from Fambridge or Burnham or Maldon (or even Heybridge Basin if you didn't mind a mile and a half walk along the canal, or taking the local taxi). Even West Mersea had its bus service to Colchester station; Brightlingsea its branchline service ('the crab and winkle express'), at Walton it was only 15 minutes' walk from the Yacht Club to the station, from Pin Mill a bus at Chelmondiston took you to Ipswich, the quay at Woodbridge was close by the station, and even Aldeburgh had its branch line train to Saxmundham on the main line.

If, when leaving the boat for a week or two, a mooring could not be hired from the local boatman, then we left her 'moored' to her anchor and kedge, big ship style. The 15 fathom or so kedge warp was bent on to the anchor cable with a rolling hitch and anchor and kedge were laid as far apart as possible up and down the edge of the channel, so that the amount of swing at the turn of each tide was minimal. The chain was paid out enough to put the hitch well below the yacht's forefoot, so that warp and chain would not get wound into an inextricable twist with the many turns of the tide.

Both our main or bower and kedge anchors were of the age-old reliable fisherman type, for Professor Taylor had not yet invented his plough or CQR (Secure) for yachts, and other patent anchors so familiar today were still in the future. The only variations then were the Nicholson (an excellent improved fisherman type), the Trotman (hinged at the crown so the upper fluke would be pulled on to the shank and less liable to foul the cable at turn of tides) and lastly the Stockless, rarely suitable for small yachts.

As laying out the anchor or kedge for mooring or when aground was a frequent occurrence with engineless yachts, a good dinghy was very necessary. Outboard motors were still heavy and highly temperamental and few cruising yachts carried them. With a well-shaped clinker-built dinghy of 8ft 6in to 10ft, we found it no hardship to row out to the anchorage, lay out the kedge, or even give the yacht a pluck in a calm under oars. And to know how to scull a dinghy with an oar through a notch in the transom – barge boat fashion – was a vital exercise when an oar was lost. (Do any of these well-meaning sailing schools teach their pupils to scull a dinghy these days, I wonder?)

Apart from the old Berthon and one or two wood-strut and canvas foldups made by their owners, there were no handy folding dinghies, and almost all cruising yachts less than, say, 32ft overall always towed their little boats. And that on a long coastal passage in all weathers made us very conscious of how best to tow the brute without losing it.

In our daily lives we rarely look closely at the familiar things that surround us, or stop to consider that in 50 years' time other people will think how lucky our generation was to enjoy such sights and sounds. In the early years of my own sailing around the East Coast in the 1920s, there was constant barge traffic between London River and the Medway and all the Essex and Suffolk estuaries.

Barges were a familiar part of our coastal scene and their sprits could be found prickling the horizon across the meadows against little quays, unloading bricks and cement, timber and barrels of beer for neighbouring villages, and taking away cargoes of farm produce. Their brown sails were to be seen

everywhere, and if you watched closely what the bargeman did
– whether they still remained at anchor under the lee of Shotley
Spit when you thought the wind was easing off and they surely
could now get away up Swin; or suddenly dropped their tops'ls
away to wind'ard and gave you warning of a heavy squall – you
had a better weather sign than any wireless forecast. And we
took it all for granted. But now, except for the handful of
privately-owned or youth sail training barges still in commis-
sion, they have all gone.

Another institution which we took for granted was the
RHYC Regatta at Harwich. This was traditionally the start of
the racing season on the East Coast, and Orwell One-Designs
and other local classes gathered here from Lowestoft,
Aldeburgh, West Mersea and Burnham. But Harwich was also
the season's first regatta for the Big Class, officially the 23-
Metres (later known as the J Class); and what yachts these
were, these sleek and graceful beauties whose sheer size would
dwarf any of today's ocean racers in Class I, and make 12-
Metres look like dinghies.

There would be the white-hulled *Lulworth*, *White Heather* and
Terpsichore together with Lipton's green *Shamrock V*. But out-
stripping them all was His Majesty's black cutter *Britannia*, a
huge beauty of 221 tons Thames Measurement, with her well-
drilled crew of twenty-one hands active about her decks as she
jockeyed (it seemed in slow motion) for the start.

Then for the season of 1923 (I think it was) Mrs Workman's
23-Metre *Nyria* took everyone aback by appearing with an
immensely lofty Marconi mast setting a jibheaded mainsail.
Nyria showed her superiority in wind'ard sailing, and within
the next few years all the other great yachts of this class were
converted from gaff rig to what inappropriately became known
as bermudian. Even the King's yacht eventually emerged as a
Marconi cutter, and never again looked so breathtaking as in
her great jackyard tops'l days.

Despite this revolution in all the racing classes, it was not
until 1930 or so that the bermudian rig started to oust the gaff

amongst the smaller cruising yachts. Until then most cruisers were gaff sloops, cutters or yawls with their jibs set flying on a bowsprit traveller ring. Many boats, however, did have the useful jib furling gear introduced by Major Wykeham Martin back in 1903. But once the early bugs of the bermudian rig were ironed out – bent mast tracks, jamming slides, weak masts, overstressed hulls and so on – the jibheaded rig proved its worth in ease of handling, lightness, lower cost and greatly improved performance to wind'ard. And in due time the post-war designs, with all inboard rig no bowsprit and well-thought-out gear, duly appeared.

On the whole the boats we sailed were of a sturdy, traditional type with a pronounced forefoot and a straight keel running aft to the heel of the rudder. Whether cutters or yawls, or with counter, transom or canoe sterns, they were generally of a healthy design which would not be found floating keel upwards whatever the weather might do to them.

Almost everywhere in East Coast anchorages you could come across lifeboats coverted to cutters or yawls of varying aesthetic degrees from gratifying to hideous. Steamships were then compelled by the Board of Trade to replace their standard clinker-built lifeboats every few years, with the result that there was always a large pool of discarded boats available at low prices. Lifeboats of 22ft to 30ft in good condition could be picked up for £25 to £45 or so, and damaged boats from £5. It was the poor fisherman's and yachtsman's way of getting a serviceable boat. The *Yachting Monthly* used to run a series of articles on conversion work, and published a booklet by Michael Verney, *Lifeboat into Yacht*, now out of print, which over some years sold several thousands. This conversion syndrome died, however, when ocean-going ships were equipped with steel, then GRP, and later aluminium alloy boats, which did not have to be replaced so often, if at all, and cheap wooden lifeboats were no longer available.

By the 1930s various yacht builders had introduced their own versions of the small two or three berth cruising yacht, and the yachtsman had a fair choice of a number of what writers sometimes described as 'pocket cruisers' or 'tabloid boats', from the current craze for reduced size or tabloid newspapers which came from America.

Many of these excellent little boats are still around, and a memory of the prices they were advertised at makes sad reading nowadays. For example, Dan Webb at Maldon offered his Blackwater sloops, sturdy little transom rounded stem 18ft (2½ ton) and 20ft (3 ton) boats at £100 and £125 each, ready to sail, without engine. Johnson & Jago at Leigh-on-Sea built their Freeman-designed 18-footers for £120; the David Hillyard 2½ ton sloop cost a few pounds more, while at Conyer in Kent, Coopers (no longer operating) produced the Conyer 6-Tonner, a nice looking 28ft canoe sterned sloop for £330 including a Stuart 8 engine. Some of these are still afloat.

About 1938, the very first attempt in this country at quantity production for yachts was made by Lockhart Marine in their Brentford furniture factory, when they jig-produced their Harrison Butler-designed Z 4-Tonners. These were fine little 22ft sloops of which some forty were built up to the War, the price including a Stuart Turner engine being £330. All these excellent and sensible little boats led the way to development by many yacht designers and builders through trial and error to produce the better cruising yachts of today.

There were still a few *steam* yachts in evidence on the East Coast in the early 1930s. Two with traditional white hulls, clipper bows and a buff funnel lay for a year or two in Burnham anchorage, while a handsome black steamer owned by a rich society woman, Miss Betty Carstairs, had her mooring off Brightlingsea. Further up Colne, where one or two yellow funnelled steam yachts were laid up, an eccentric American, Bayard Brown, kept his big yacht permanently in steam but never, so far as I know, got under way.

Moored in the Colne also before the Hitler War was a lovely period piece in the black-hulled clipper-bowed schooner *Tamessis*, of some 120 tons built in 1875, which was often to be met sailing around the coast. Broken up during the war, her capstan now rests in Mersea Museum.

Motor-cruisers were already fairly numerous, but mostly of a traditional low profile type with narrow displacement hulls and teak deckhouses; the high-speed cruisers, shaped like pointed shoe boxes and capped by towering upperworks and a flying bridge, were yet to be ushered in with the post-war explosion of 'leisure facilities' and waterlike wealth.

Although in those days anchorages near any hard could become congested, if you chose your favourite one further down river, say, it was not so likely as today that some clot would come and drop his hook within yards of your boat. Most cruising men also frapped their halyards, either around the mast or tied out to the shrouds, for the night as a matter of course; today's clanging and tinkling halyards, and ensigns left out all night, wouldn't have been tolerated. Brought up in an older school, perhaps, the average owner of those days usually observed a yachtsman's recognised courtesy code.

Perhaps the most noticeable difference between those far-off days and the yachting scene today is in the sheer numbers of pleasure craft of all types now competing for manoeuvring space around our coasts. From the windows of my house at West Mersea I can look across the mouth of the Blackwater to Sales Point, and on any fine Sunday in summer I can count 300 or more boats in sight and under way. The animated scene sometimes resembles a boat lake on a busy Bank Holiday.

This, I think, is all to the good that so many people are now able to enjoy their much greater leisure and affluence in this healthiest of sports, messing about in boats.

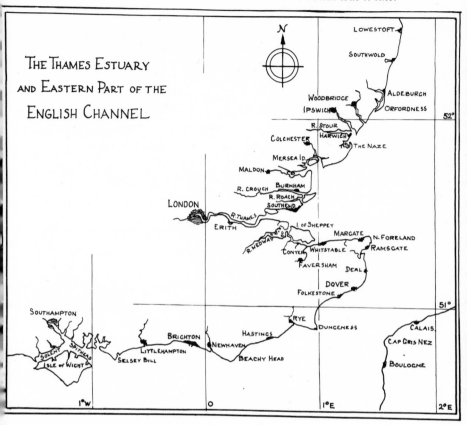

[The Thames Estuary and
Eastern part of the English Channel]

– 2 –
Too much of a fair wind

Apart from the chance of a sail round the coast – even though it was still early in March – there was the added lure of being *paid* to do it. Derek's finances as a young City clerk were at their usual low ebb, while I was still a struggling freelance journalist and barely making ends meet. A little money would be very welcome.

We were glad, therefore, to accept a job to sail the *Arabel* from Walton Backwaters, where she had been laid up, round to Gravesend where her new owner had his mooring. He had explained with an expression on his face of profound regret that, much as he would love to have come, business commitments, y'know, prevented it.

"It shouldn't take you chaps long", he assured us. "After all, it's only seventy miles, and if this northerly wind lasts it'll be downhill all the way." He made it sound like an easy toboggan ride.

When on the Friday evening we boarded the yacht in the Twizzle from her rather leaky old dinghy, *Arabel* turned out to be quite a nice-looking, white-painted, 6-tonne cutter, about 9.5 metres on deck and in shape like a somewhat refined smack, with a long flat counter aft. The owner had told us that she drew "about four foot six" (although at the time I suspected he was being unduly modest about her draught), that her sails and gear were in "tiptop order", and, quite uncommon for that date (it was 1925), that she had an auxiliary petrol engine, called a Seal.

Once we had lit the gimballed lamp, stowed our kit and started up the galley stove for warmth and a brew-up, it was this mechanical wonder that took our attention. Viewed from above when the cabin steps were removed, it looked surprisingly like an electric motor, and it took us a little while to realise that what leered up at our puzzled gaze was the crankcase. The owner had doubtless assumed we were well acquainted with the unorthodox Seal engine, which had been designed in the first year or two of this century, with its cylinder inverted and underneath the crankcase. It was thus shaped so that it could fit into the deep and sharply veed runs of old timers like *Arabel*.

It took us an hour after supper to get the brute to turn at all with the starting handle, but sweat and perseverence won in the end, and the sound of its loud 'crump-crump', even if not exactly regular, gave us a feeling of confidence of being able to get out of the Pye channel against the wind early in the morning. It was, in fact, Derek who had worked out the tides in the train coming down from London.

"Look, MG", he had said, "I reckon our best course tomorrow won't be through the Wallet to the Spitway buoy and then into the Swin, but if this northerly wind holds it will pay us to go straight out to the NE Gunfleet buoy, and then to square away for the Barrow Deep with the first of the flood under us. We'll want to be at that turning point so we don't waste a minute of the south-going flood tide, not a moment after low water, and that tomorrow morning at the NE Gunfleet will be – let's see – about 0800. If we can rely on the auxiliary getting us out to the Pye End buoy in, let's say one hour from the mooring, and it's then a broad reach out to the Gunfleet, say just under two hours, then I reckon we ought to be away at 5am sharp."

And so we should have been. We were up and breakfasted before there was more than a glimmer of dawn in the sky, but the upside-down Seal refused to start again. Swing and curse as we would, and we did, dry the plug again on the primus, and swing, swing again, the sullen mass of rusty iron refused even a morning smoker's cough.

"Never can rely on engines," exclaimed my shipmate, but not so politely. "Come on, we'll get sail on her."

In a mild rage, which at least kept us warm in the cold morning air, we tucked a reef in the mainsail (for the wind was still fresh and keen from the north-east) and setting the stays'l and the No 2 jib half way along the bowsprit, smack-fashion, we dropped the mooring. But working on the engine had cost us more than a precious hour of our ebb, and when we had turned down the Pye Channel in short tacks it was already getting on for low water. Once or twice as we beat to windward of the Pye End buoy our keel thudded heavily on the granite hard sands, rattling the lee shrouds. We held our breath for a minute or two, wondering if we were going to get across these flats, but with her sheets pinned in on port tack *Arabel* mercifully leant over to a harder squall with her covering board awash, and managed to work out to sea with her keel just clear of the bottom.

Funny how it is, when you are desperately trying to save every moment of a tide, that the time appears to race by. It seemed only minutes before Derek said "We'll have to harden in sheets again, MG, and head her up a bit more. The flood's already begun – this wind may be helping it – and it's setting us steadily to leeward of the buoy."

The words were hardly out of his mouth when the wind came in a stronger gust and laid the old cutter over with her lee rail under. A heavy dollop of spray leapt over the weather rail and struck us in the face. With both feet braced against the lee coaming I could hardly hold her (neither of us had yet learnt to use tiller lines to ease the strain) and it was a relief to round up with the jib aback, muzzle the flogging stays'l and lash it to the bitts, and tie down the second reef in the mainsail.

As we bore away again with the sheets hardened in there followed a resounding thud from up forward, and the jib

['Too occupied . . . to shout a witty
repartee']

started crackling in the wind like a machine gun. Its tack, together with the iron ring traveller on the bowsprit, had slid aft almost to the stemhead, and the sail had slackened into a belly which was flogging as though demented.

"One darn thing after another," exclaimed Derek at the helm. "That outhaul's carried away."

There seemed no doubt as to who was to go out along the bowsprit to re-reeve the line, and I donned my seaboots so as to keep at least my feet dry. The rope, I found, had parted at the splice where it was attached to the traveller ring; it had thoughtfully run forward through the sheave at the outboard end of the bowsprit and was trailing in the water from its cleat by the stemhead.

"I'll just jill her along so you don't get too wet, I hope," grinned my shipmate, but I was too occupied balancing with legs astride the bowsprit as I inched my way along towards the end to be able to turn round and shout one of those witty repartees I can sometimes think of minutes afterwards. The old lean-bowed *Arabel* was not plunging too much too often, however, and only my boots resting on the bobstay were getting a regular ducking.

But as I struggled to insert the frayed end of the outhaul from underneath into the sheave hole, my weight at the end of the ten-foot spar, together with the inevitable three seas bigger than the others, combined to duck me twice with a crash up to the waist. Whatever cry of sympathy – or shout of laughter – might have come from the helm was lost in my own loud cussing as I worked my way backwards to the stem, clambered aboard, and made the outhaul fast to the traveller again.

By the time the jib was reset with the traveller half-way along the bowsprit again the NE Gunfleet was well to windward of us. But Derek held the yacht hard on the wind, bucking the cross tide for the time being, and slowly, slowly the striped buoy drew abreast of us, reeling and twisting as the sluicing tide poured round its sides. At last we were able to bear away on port gybe and head for the mouth of the Thames with the spring tide carrying us along.

The sun came out from behind the morning clouds and began to cast a pale light over the vibrant scene, picking out the colour in the sandy green seas, and catching here and there the dazzling whiteness of breaking crests. Coming our way out of the London River a small coasting steamer with a tall black and white funnel forged past us, heading north with the spray bursting in white clouds on to her fo'c's'le head and washing along her rusty black sides. If anything, her bluff disdain made the short seas look even more angry.

Away to starboard, perhaps two miles, the old red pile lighthouse on the edge of the Gunfleet Sands drifted slowly past, and as we ran down towards the Barrow Deep light vessel we could see the water cascading from her great hawsepipes as her bluff bows rose and fell. One by one the numbered buoys of the channel were ticked off the chart, Number 5 a black speck to starboard, Number 6 a red and white check cage tossing by to port; away to starboard again the East Barrow beacon over the sands passing in transit with the conical Number 7 buoy, and then the big Number 8 Barrow reeling towards our port rigging with the spray washing over its iron sides.

Bright red against the green and white of the seas, the hull of the Mid Barrow light vessel lay ahead, slewed partly away from the wind, and rolling slowly.

"That darned lightship's just on the turn." Derek spoke with some disgust. "We've had all the fair tide we're going to get today."

For a time it didn't seem to matter, for this wind was steadily becoming stronger, and we told ourselves it just couldn't be fairer for our passage. *Arabel* was beginning to sheer about as the following seas rose under her long flat counter, and we were obliged to take shorter spells at the tiller, for the old girl at times was the very devil to hold.

As the ebb began to run more strongly the seas became noticeably higher and steeper, and their white crests were beginning to overtake us with an angrier hiss. Once or twice the

['*Arabel* was beginning to sheer about']

yacht's counter came down on them with a thud that set the shrouds rattling, and we wondered silently if one of the seams near the rudder trunk might get opened and start leaking badly. But neither of us gave vent to our thoughts at the time.

"The dinghy doesn't seem too happy."

We had let the little clinker-built boat out to the full length of its painter, which we had noted was sensibly made fast to an eyebolt half-way down the stem, and it was towing heavily, suggesting there was already a good deal of water in her. But this didn't prevent the seas from picking her up and surging her forward until the little boat was under the counter or almost alongside.

"Know something" asked Derek ruefully. "We forgot to rig a drag line to the stern thwart before we started."

"But what with? There doesn't seem to be a bit of spare line in any of the lockers. Every darn thing's rotten in this ship."

Arabel was roaring along about as fast as she could go under the press of her double-reefed main and small jib (how thankful we now were that we hadn't set the big jib at the start) and she was beginning to take charge. It was while Derek was straining at the helm that a huge crest broke over the stern and deposited the bow of the dinghy with a crunch on to the taffrail.

For a moment the boat hung there, then slid off and dropped astern to the length of its painter. There was a muffled thud and the painter slackened as the dinghy receded astern behind the next comber. The frayed end of the broken painter was only a few feet away.

"We'll have to pick the damn thing up."

Both thinking unprintable words, we overhauled the mainsheet, strained in the jib, and brought the yacht round close-hauled on the port tack. It was only then we realised how hard it was blowing, for *Arabel* just lay over, burying her lee deck while the water slopped over the lee coaming.

With spring ebb now under her lee bow, she drove her whipping bowsprit into the seas, tossing the water aside from her foredeck as her bows lifted over every crest, working her way gamely to windward. We had already lost sight of our dinghy amidst the white crests, but after two short boards Derek spotted her, and ten minutes later he had skilfully brought the yacht just to windward of the little boat.

With jib hauled aback and tiller held down to the lee coaming with a loop of mainsheet, we grabbed the dinghy and got hold of the rest of its painter. There was a lot of water washing under the thwarts, and while Derek held her alongside I managed to get several bucketfuls back into the sea before bending the bucket's lanyard on to the after thwart as a stern drogue. It must slow the yacht somewhat, but at least we reckoned it would keep the dinghy astern.

As we were about to bear away again Derek pointed up at the mains'l. "Look there," he exclaimed. "That's not nice, is it?"

A foot-long tear had started in the leech cloth above the second cringle. For the few seconds we looked fascinated at it the tear crept upward towards the third and last row of reef points.

"Rotten canvas," was his comment. "We'll have to tuck in our last reef, and pretty damn quick!"

When I had clambered awkwardly to the mast and with topping lift tautened eased off the main halyard, Derek braced himself with feet well apart on the pitching taffrail, struggling to reeve the leechline through the maddened cringle like a palsied old woman threading her needle. But his language was far from ladylike.

It took us perhaps half an hour to get that third reef down and the pendants tied, but at last it was done and the tear in the canvas relieved of strain. Once more *Arabel* headed for the Thames, more snugly rigged now and better under control; but when we had time to look around us and notice how the surface of the Barrow Deep was covered in white foam, and the very crests of the seas appeared to be levelled and blown to leeward in fine spume by the wind, we reckoned it must be blowing a full gale.

I clambered below to try to brew up some cocoa on the galley stove and found an inch or two of water surging about the floor. Derek, the imperturbable shipmate, took the news calmly as I erupted back into the cockpit.

"Better man the bilge-pump," he said "while I steer."

It took a hundred and forty strokes of the deck pump to clear her, and we discussed the probable cause – those heavy bumps on the sand by the Pye End buoy, or just working badly in this seaway? As I returned below and managed to produce two good mugs of steaming sweetened cocoa and something to munch, the thought niggled at the backs of our minds that the leak could grow much worse in weather like this. And I made it my duty to work the pump every half-hour or so.

Despite the way the yacht was bustling through the water the dinghy again came running up on a high steep sea until it was alongside the cockpit, and we saw that the bucket's lanyard had parted, the drogue gone. When the little boat dropped back and the painter tautened there was a sharp crack, and once again the dinghy was lost behind the seas astern.

We said nothing as I began to haul in what was left of the painter to find, gyrating and flapping on the end like a fish, the dinghy's stem. It had pulled clean out from the aged plank ends!

The wind was so strong now – we told each other it must be a full Force 8, as though that did something for our shaky morale – that it was all we could do to hold *Arabel* before the wind and seas without a disasterous gybe, which we feared could bring her mast down. I even felt better during my tricks at the helm, for sitting inside the cockpit while Derek was steering I could watch the seas curling up astern, and some of them rose so high and fell over with such angry noise – like an express train roaring through a station – I felt that sooner or later one must tumble on to our counter and fill the cockpit. And we had no bucket now for bailing.

In the gusts the mast was whipping and shaking the rusty shrouds while the boom would lift high as though intent on a Chinese gybe. We were both by now thoroughly wet and cold and tired from all our exertions, and so far as I was concerned very frightened of what part of our rotten gear might go next. There was still something like 25 miles of angry white water to go against this ebb to Gravesend, and it would be dark in less than two hours. By common consent we steered for the entrance of the Medway, deciding to spend the night at anchor under the lee of Sheerness.

Seldom have I let go an anchor with greater relief, when we rounded up in the comparative calm behind the great fort, nor settled more happily to a hot supper in the cabin lamplight, as I did that evening. Even pumping the bilge dry for the nth time was no longer a chore.

Next morning the sky was fine and clear, the gale had blown itself out, and there was less than a whole sail breeze, still from the north-east. With such a tear in our mainsail we dared not shake out any of the reefs, and had to be content to sail slowly up on the tide through Sea Reach and Lower Hope, picking up a mooring off Gravesend about midday.

The new owner, in bowler hat and office suit and with mac over the arm, was rowed out from the landing in a longshoreman's boat.

"What kept you," he asked as he clambered awkwardly aboard. "I waited for you yesterday. And where's the dinghy?"

We both took a deep breath before telling him, and handing him what was left of the dinghy's stem. And some time later, in the train for London Bridge, Derek remarked with a grin: "Fancy the old so-and-so trying to knock a quid off our fee for losing his dinghy. I must say, MG, it's a hard way to earn a few pounds, but by Jove we did have a fine sail, didn't we?"

– 3 –
A cruise without an engine

The flood tide had another two hours yet to run, and as we anged alongside our little ship in the dinghy the cracked chimes of the town clock striking three travelled clearly across the water. It was mid-week at the end of June, and the Burnham waterfront was almost deserted. Even the usual group of peak-capped experts had dispersed: too early, perhaps, after their dinnertime to resume their perch along the river wall.

A light north-easterly breeze ruffled the water, filled our tan sails and began to drive our white hull over the tide. Still swaying with indignation at his unceremonious dismissal from the foredeck, our mooring buoy dropped astern, to become blended with the forest of masts and hulls of the seven hundred or more yachts that filled the anchorage. From the sounds of opening locker doors and drawers below, I gathered my crew were both stowing their gear, for we had all three arrived half an hour before, hot and crumpled from the train journey down from London.

As I eased off the mainsheet a little and felt *Nightfall* surge ahead more strongly as a lively puff filled her sails, I could not help thinking how good it was to have two congenial shipmates like Marty and Nevill aboard with me, a week's holiday before us, and from the Met office a promise of cyclonic weather. My companions were both experienced in the ways of little ships, for they shared a fine deep-draught cruising cutter which they kept on the Solent, and they had elected to desert their own boat in order to join me for some creek-crawling on the East Coast.

Nightfall was my eleventh small ship, and up to that time the most satisfactory of them all – for my modest type of cruising. Even after two years of ownership she continued to surprise me with her general all-round qualities for exploring this part of the coast, as she had comfortable accommodation, standing headroom in the cabin, a fast and surprisingly dry hull, a draught with her long iron keel of only one metre, and an engaging ability to look after herself, hove-to or sailing with tiller pegged, for hours on end. The mahogany and beechwood panelling in her cabin, the chest of drawers in the fo'c'sle, and the galley between that and the cabin reflected her Edwardian upbringing. In short, she was a comfortable old 9.5 metre shoal draught gaff cutter with a nice nature.

It had been our intention to spend this first night in the Roach, and to cross the Estuary to the Kentish shore next day. But this breeze was waking up, as it so often does on the approach to high water (although Met people will tell you this is nonsense – there's no explanation for it), it was only just past spring tides, and it occurred to me that there would be enough water in Havengore creek for our shallow draught to slip across the Maplins, and perhaps even make the Swale before dark. It would save hours in working the next ebb round the Whitaker Spit and back up the Swin with the first of the flood on the morrow, and would then give us a full day's start on our short cruise.

The breeze continued to be kind to us and followed us as we rustled up the Roach, through the Narrow Gut creek and under the raised iron bridge spanning the Havengore Gut between the mainland and Foulness island. Sounding our way over the shallows with the pole and finding a foot or so beneath our keel, we sailed over three miles of the hard, flat Maplins until the water suddenly deepened and we were in the main ship channel. With the almost two metres of draught of their own ship it was an uncanny experience for my crew.

"It's like sailing on roller skates," Neville observed as he emerged from the cabin with tea, plates of cut bread and butter and boiled eggs. "And the land astern of us looks just as flat as these sands – not much more than a pencil line."

Out here amongst the big ships steaming in and out of London's river the wind became mildly boisterous for a while, and *Nightfall* bustled happily across the ten miles of the Estuary towards the eastern end of the Isle of Sheppy, while we let her steer herself and bent our attention to the serious business of consuming a hearty late tea. The long cockpit was well adapted for having meals in the open.

The tide had turned by now and the ebb was pouring out into the North Sea, so that our course lay obliquely to clear the end of the Spile sand. The north-easterly breeze was turning the water into a frolicsome mood, and *Nightfall*'s motion was lively as she sped before the short seas that welled up under her quarter. In due course we were butting the strong tide that was sluicing out of the East Swale, and the breeze noticed that high water had come and gone and took the opportunity to ease off.

It was already dusk, and night threatened to close down, leaving us at the entrance to this unlighted haven. For half an hour Shell Ness hovered off our starboard beam, hardly moving in the direction we tried to will it, while on the other side of us the lights of Whitstable and Herne Bay came out, one by one, winking at us across the fast uncovering flats. Against the land we could just make out the Whitstable pilot ketch, black-hulled and sturdy as a ship, where she lifted and fell at her station.

There was still an appreciable swell rolling in from seaward, and the peace of the river, still a long way beyond our bowsprit, tantalised us with its promise of a quiet night – if we could get there. There was too much of a wind-against-the-tide jobble here to make a quiet anchorage.

"If only we had an engine . . . " began Marty, and we all

gave a hollow laugh. Their own heavy Kelvin would have pushed us up at a rate of knots, but *Nightfall*'s original engine had become filled with water, rusted solid and been removed, and I was sailing her as an engineless boat for the second year in succession.

Perhaps hearing our muttered prayers, the wind revived for a time, and by degrees we edged our way against the tide until Shell Ness was astern, and we crept round the fringe of the yellow Horse Sand that now arched its smooth back above the water in the twilight. Below half a dozen yachts' riding lights, which appeared one by one from round the point of land, we achieved our slow and patient arrival, taking it in turns to go below and eat a late meal that began heavily and trailed away into cheese and biscuits and jam and merged into the wash-up bowl, as boat meals underway tend to do. And it was gone 11 o'clock before our own anchor was let go and the riding light hung up on the forestay. We were tired but supremely happy with our first day's venture: it was a fair start.

Morning and a bright sun and clear sky showed us the charms of this anchorage: the distant fields in the south beyond Faversham and Sittingbourne, and the grassy mound of Sheppy above the hard, with the white farmhouse and the old Ferry Inn at its foot. Marty looked round at our few neighbouring yachts.

"Why, an anchorage like this," he exclaimed, "in the Solent would be *packed* with craft of all kinds and outboard motors on the go all the time! It's so peaceful here."

This part of the coast was entirely new to my Solent crew, and, in deference to their keenness to explore farther up the winding Swale, I gladly agreed to give up this day to some peaceful pottering. The morning's breeze was still in the north, and soon after low water when *Nightfall* was lying head to wind we set the mainsail, broke out the hook, unrolled the jib and wended our way up river between the green fields of Sheppey on the one hand and the land to the south, where tall chimneys of the various cement works drew a pale haze over the countryside, on the other.

Past Elmley Ferry, and off the mouth of the creek leading up to the chimneys and works and houses of Sittingbourne, we forebore to go on tacking up the next narrow reach, but put the ship round to return close-hauled on her tracks against the flood. As we came abreast of Fowley Island again Nevill studied the chart on the cockpit seat.

"What's Conyer like?" he asked. "Irving marks here a dock, a boatyard and an inn. Would there be enough water for us in the creek yet?"

"Good idea," agreed Marty. "We might see if the inn could give us a bite to eat. It's nearly 12 o'clock and I'm beginning to feel really peckish. What about it, Skipper?"

Bearing away behind the island we dropped the lead and found the water shoaling to a metre and a bit. The mainsail was lowered smartly, and as *Nightfall* glided silently to a stop almost in the entrance to the creek, we rolled up the jib and dropped anchor well to one side with a few fathoms of chain. In a few minutes we were in the dinghy pulling the half-mile or so between the high muddy banks towards the head of the creek.

John Irving's *Rivers and Creeks of the Thames Estuary* was quite right about the facilities and delights to be had at Conyer, for there lay ahead a motley assortment of craft of all sorts and sizes by the boatyard, while farther up four or five barges proudly held their sprits against the blue sky, and above their brailed tan sails the bobs, their owners' houseflags, fluttered in the breeze at their mastheads. Beyond the ancient quay stood the welcome sight of the old inn.

From the window of the bar parlour we were able to look at all the boats, contentedly munching good fresh bread and cheese while listening to the voices of the knot of locals at the bar. With this incursion of strangers into their domain, and after a suitable pause in talk while they eyed the newcomers, the old salts launched into the age-old custom of locals in waterside pubs the world over, recounting tall yarns of gales and shipwrecks and derring-do for the benefit of visitors.

Nevill, giving us a surreptitious wink and wearing his most innocent expression, encouraged them with exclamations of "ah, oh, you don't say, but what danger to face, well I'm blowed", and suchlike.

Ordering pints of mild and bitter all round, he warmed up to the occasion and asked: "Do you every get any wrecks on this coast?" and buried his face in his own pint mug to stop laughing. It was too good an opportunity to let slip, and one of the salts set sail with a yarn that went something like this:

"Wrecks, sir? Why, only last winter there was this yer schooner, sir, hailin' out of Belfast, loaded with plank wood from the Baltic, she was, wot drove on to the end of the Columbine. It blew a full gale o'wind from the nor'ard as night come on with a great sea a-breakin' over the banks, an' me and my pal Fred 'ere see her come fast in the breakers out there on that spit. Fred and me, we took our bo't and rowed out to them through all them seas – and they was all a-breakin' – it was a mighty hard row, I can tell you sir – oh, thanks mister, I don't mind if I do – and when we got alongside we see the whole crew was lyin' about in the scuppers, they was all too drunk to do a thing. We couldn't see the captain, reckon he was in his cabin prayin' like. We got aboard and you could tell by the way she was movin' that she would be liftin' on the tide any minute, but we didn't let on. So Fred 'ere, he shins aloft and sets the only sail what hadn't blowed away, the lower topsail it was, and with that she started to come off of the sand, bumpin' fit to bust her timbers, she was.

"It was pitch dark by now, sir, and you couldn't see yer hand before yer face, but Fred 'ere and me, we know our way in past the Ness. I had the wheel, and when she at last come free we steer her right into the river and brung up inside the Horse. You should've seen them Paddies' faces when daylight come and they could see land all round 'em and the ship at anchor, quiet-like. "Mither of God," they hollered, "we've been saved." "Aye," I says, "and by honest Protestants!"

It was indeed a place to dream away a warm summer's

afternoon, and my crew were as reluctant as I was to be dragged out into the fresh air when the pub closed. So reluctant were they that I might borrow with full apologies from Chaucer:

> *Bifel that, in that seson on a day*
> *At Conyere, in the Swale, our good shippe lay;*
> *At noon was come into that hostelrye*
> *Three shippmen gently in a companye;*
> *But from that hostelrye they wende*
> *Noisome and disorderlye they were sende!*

On the stroke of 6 o'clock next morning we congratulated ourselves on getting underway at the appointed hour, turning out of the Swale on the ebb against a light breeze a little east of north. The Whitstable fleet of oyster dredgers was out in force – fine sturdy cutters with their topsails set, a ketch or two, and several motor craft – and, as we wended our way through them, their crews gave us a hearty wave. From about a half mile off the end of Whitstable Street, that finger of gravel and sand which stretches almost a mile out from the beach, forming a natural hard for the fishermen, we were just able to lay our course along the coast towards the Copperas Channel. The sun was well above the horizon, the breeze seemed steady if a little shy, and the water was surprisingly clear and smooth: what more could innocent mariners desire?

It was our intention to make the North Foreland by slack water and to take the south-going stream around the corner into Ramsgate or Pegwell Bay. But when the twin towers of Reculver were almost abeam a mile and a half distant, our fickle north-easterly breeze began to falter and fade away. It was almost at this same spot, I recalled, that last year with my old friend Bill on board with me we had had much the same experience. Then it had been much later in the day, and with hardly a breath to interest our sails and the tide beginning to run foul, we had had to spend the night at anchor near the edge of the Margate Hook sand (see *The First of the Tide*).

The calm remained with us until the tide turned and we had to let go the hook to avoid being set back. It gave us an opportunity to dive in turn into the shockingly cold water with cries of spurious delight ("Come on in, it's luverly – urrgh!") and to enjoy a leisurely lunch in the cockpit afterwards. At least, as Marty pointed out, this was civilised yachting and made to be enjoyed.

It began to look as though last year's experience out here was to repeat itself with a prolonged calm, but no two days when sailing are exactly the same, and by mid-afternoon catspaws reaching in patches across the water from the direction of the shore brought the first puffs of a breeze from the south-east. Soon it filled in with more strength, until there appreared hints of a white cap or two, and with the anchor aboard again and all plain sail set *Nightfall* leant gratefully to the breeze and began to make her way steadily over the tide. The Reculver towers dropped astern in the faint mist and gradually the broken skyline of Birchington, then Westgate, emerged and passed away abeam.

By 1900 hours Margate pier loomed up broad off the starboard bow, and we held a confab. With the tide against us for at least another two hours, and this south-easter a foul wind once we turned the corner of the North Foreland, we should have little chance of making Ramsgate for the night. We could, of course, drop our hook closer inshore from where we now were, but there was still a restless swell making in from the North Sea, an aftermath of the past few days of north-easterly winds, and this would make any open roadstead berth an uncomfortable one.

"Let's go into the harbour," we agreed, "and see what it's like. The tide must have made plenty by now for our draught."

The warning notes in *The Pilot's Guide* which had put Bill and me off entering Margate the previous year ('There is little shelter and yachtsmen are not recommended to enter without special reason') were forgotten – or maybe we felt we had enough special reasons, wanting a quiet night – and in due course *Nightfall* worked her way in short tacks past the long outer jetty, the breeze becoming warmer as we entered the harbour with all the scents of a seaside town.

"I can smell fish and chips," said Marty, "and sticks of Margate rock. I'm feeling peckish again."

Amongst the mixed bag of craft nestling closely in the harbour we spied a clear berth at the quay wall, and with sails dropped *Nightfall* obediently carried her way alongside. In a few minutes my excellent crew had lines out and fenders in place and a masthead preventer to one of the bollards. Looking around at the fishing boats, the chains of coloured lights, the people on the quay and the busy traffic beyond, it was difficult not to imagine that this was a Continental port.

But we were all tired from the fresh air and the long day's activities, and resisted the urge to scale the slippery rungs of the quay ladder and see what bright lights this queen of watering places could offer simple shipmen. As the tide fell we sat in the cockpit in contemplation, attending to our lines until our keel was resting on the bottom, and *Nightfall* was leaning firmly against her fenders. Then as the water ebbed away in the darkness and the mud became uncovered we were again reminded that we could well be in a foreign port, as Nevill pointed out.

"My lord, doesn't the mud pong. It reminds me of Calais!"

"It's probably only the ozone they boast about," suggested Marty, but with one accord we followed him into the cabin, closing the doors behind us, while my companions challenged the smell outside with the thicker, but slightly less noisome, atmosphere produced by their pipes. In time sleep overcame one after the other, and all was still and quiet.

Nothing came to disturb us until the tide, welling into the harbour at dawn, lifted *Nightfall* gently and set her rolling against the fenders with sleep-shattering groans and creaks. And at a quarter past six there was not only activity on board but even good humour over the breakfast table. Good manners and pleasant banter at that hour in the morning: such can be the influence of a happy ship's company.

It was getting on for high water, and though from our berth behind the quay we could feel only the motion, our burgee was fluttering to tell us that there was a snoring breeze from north-west outside. This slight swell was running round the pier head and making our ship restless to be on our way. By seven o'clock she was tacking out past the outer jetty and sensing the first of the frolicsome wavelets. As I stood by the mast coiling halyards and Nevill at the helm headed her east-wards towards the Longnose buoy, there was a joyous roar of the bow wave, a sound we had missed for the past two days. By common consent we were bound for Dunkerque.

Past the cliffs of the Foreland we gybed and stood gaily on for the Elbow buoy while the sun rose into an almost cloudless sky. It was a joyous morning to be underway, and with this fair wind our spirits rose to such an extent that someone, momen-tarily forgetting the ageless superstition of those who are at sea in a sailing ship, remarked that at this rate we might be in Dunkerque before dark. Woe is man who so tempts the gods.

The fresh wind hurried us on while we remarked the colour of the steep cliffs by Broadstairs with the morning sun full on them, every outcrop and cleft and wavy stratum etched in light and shade as though it was a painting. The horizon had disap-peared and it seemed there was some mist out there on the sea, and to confirm our suspicions presently came the shrill howl of the North Goodwin foghorn to dominate the rest of our day. But our attention was arrested by the sight of a four-masted barque away off our port bow which had come out of the mist as she was in the slow business of tacking about a mile away. A steam tug was standing by as we watched the barque come about and back her mainyards, slowly losing her way as she now lay hove-to. The tug ranged almost alongside, and then as she drew cautiously ahead taking up the slack of the long tow line, the barque's crew were aloft on the yards furling her sails, one by one. It was an unforgettable sight, all too soon lost in the all-prevailing mistiness.

"I think the sun's going to gobble up all the wind."

Nevill at the tiller uttered all our thoughts, for we had already sensed a change of rhythm, a less urgent note in the bow wave, and less fussiness from the dinghy. This wind was indeed dying, and by 10:30, when the distant cliffs had disappeared in the encroaching fog, our brave little north-westerly had given up the ghost and left us wallowing and rolling, and our mainboom crashing and banging in an oily swell. The regular three groans of the North Goodwin only reminded us at minute intervals that we were drifting on the tide almost invisible in the fog. All around us the sea seemed to move and heave in an oily calm, and to stop the mainsheet crashing back and forth across the horse like a dog shaking a rat the sheet was hauled taut and belayed. *Nightfall* didn't like it any more than we did, for her motion at times verged on the hysterical as she dipped and rolled and curtsied to the swell.

I was thinking of the last occasion on which I had sailed this way, and how very different the scene had appeared then. It had been six years previously, when Peter and I in our 8-ton *Wilful* were on our abortive cruise down Channel, and had just come across the Estuary in the darkness, running before a strong north-easterly breeze with breaking seas. Much had happened since then. *Wilful* had been sold and Peter was now married to a highly successful marine artist, with her own boat, a 32ft Falmouth yawl, in which she was training girl apprentices in the art of seamanship and cruising in small yachts in the West Country: a pioneer, in fact, in the Sea Rangers style.

"What's that other sound?" Marty was saying as he held up a finger. Through the mist it came again: four unearthly grunts like Zulu warriors at a war dance. They were coming across the water somewhere away to the south.

"That'll be the East Goodwin," said Nevill with his finger on the chart. "It must be about eight miles away, on the outer edge of the sands. That's a place to avoid, even in a calm like this, eh Skipper?"

As the morning passed into afternoon the tide was carrying

us in a general north-easterly direction as the slowly changing bearing on both the North and East Goodwin light vessels' diaphones told us. Towards low water a long patch of disturbed water on our beam looked as if it was steadily coming towards us, a mass of little waves like the confused wash of a passing ship, but perhaps over an area half a mile across. We passed through it, our indignant cutter tossing her head and lurching with surprise, and then watched the overfalls fade into the mist on the other side.

"This must be some uneven ground, hereabouts," we remarked, "to cause that amount of a jobble in a flat calm like this. It just says 'overfalls' on the chart, here. Shouldn't like to go through them in a gale of wind, would you?"

As if to give us a reminder, in case we hadn't noticed the overfalls the first time, when the tide turned and the flood set in, what should it do two hours later but carry us back through the same patch of unruly water. As our little ship danced and cavorted and slammed about a second time it made us feel like the Ancient Mariner. But the tide carried us on, towards the south this time, and still there was not a breath of wind, while the sun beat down through the mist. The sound of the East Goodwin's four grunts passed slowly to the westward of us and we estimated that we must be heading almost for the middle of the Dover Straits, and yearned to get steerage way on the boat.

And then, praise be, it came. Dark areas of ripples across the water from a south-westerly direction brought us the first breaths of a little breeze. The mainsheet was eased, the head-sails gently filled, life at last stirred in the tiller, and *Nightfall* began to move happily through the water.

"This isn't strong enough to push us over the flood towards Dunkerque," I suggested. "But we can just lay close-hauled for Dover with the tide under us, and get in before dark. What do you say?"

There was no dissent, and *Nightfall* continued to slip almost silently through the water with her dinghy whispering astern, while the double wail of the South Goodwin's foghorn came steadily nearer and then passed, invisible, away to starboard. The evening wore on with the breeze growing rather more fitful and our patience wearing a little thin as we scanned the fog to leeward for a sight of the land.

"Behold, oh Skipper," cried Nevill with a dramatic gesture on the foredeck, "yonder I spy the South Foreland."

Yes, there loomed the bluff cliffs, just discernible through the mist. They looked so close that one expected to close with them at any moment, until we saw a steamer creeping along at their foot. It was in fact almost two hours later before we could discern the eastern entrance to Dover harbour a mile or so away from our bowsprit. It would not be long now, we said, but we'd not learnt our lesson yet. Almost immediately our nice little sailing breeze faltered, veered more into the west, and fell light again.

We bore away a little, heading inshore as close-hauled as we could take her, and as we slowly approached those forbidding chalk cliffs in a slight rolling swell we could see that the east-going steam had begun, and we were being set back already too strongly to use our sweep. It was no place to anchor with a swell amongst so many rocks, and it began to look as if we should be compelled to spend part of the night drifting helplessly back through the Downs. Never before had I felt the absence of a willing engine under the cockpit as I did just then: yet my excellent crew made not one comment on the matter. Perhaps they were as speechless as I felt.

Dusk was spreading over the calm water when we spied a small white motor cruiser coming along from the east, whose skipper evidently understood our plight. After assuring us this was simply a case of one yachtsman helping another and not a matter of salvage, he towed us in to a quiet berth in the Camber, and we blessed his kindness and all fellow yachtsmen who willingly go to the assistance of others.

Another early morning start saw us underway with a brisk whole sail breeze from out of its old quarter, the north-east. With our course roughly south-east our little ship was surging over the short seas, while we sang happily at our various tasks. It seemed almost too good to be true to have a soldier's wind to take us over to the other side, and while my companions steered and looked after the sheets, I busied myself with rule, pencil and paper beneath the cockpit floorboards.

Until this little cruise, having no engine in *Nightfall* had been no hardship during all the weekends and summer holidays we had been together over these past two years. Indeed, from the time I first began sailing on the Orwell in the old straight-stem cutter, and over the next five years when I had owned four boats, one after the other, not one of them had possessed an auxiliary motor. It had been a tough school, but a fine way of learning how to handle boats and make every possible use of winds and tides and eddies, as in the days before engines had been invented. And, I recollected, never once had we failed to get the boat back to her moorings on a Sunday evening (or early tide Monday morning!) over those first few years. The tides had ruled our every plan, and if to get home on time it meant catching a 4 o'clock tide in the morning, then that was the time we were up and underway: and what heavenly moments they could be on a fine morning, as dawn was breaking, the breeze was soft and gentle, and you could listen to the cries of the gulls and the waders across the flats.

But these few days of drifting becalmed with Marty and Nevill had brought out how exasperating such cyclonic weather could become without the aid of an 'iron topsail' when trying to make a passage. Seamen in the days of sail possessed more patience than our generation when they were hold up by calms, and remained at anchor for days – sometimes weeks – waiting for a change in the wind. Today, most of us cruising types have only a limited number of days, not even weeks, for our holiday cruises, and patience and apathy in the face of unco-operative elements is not a common virtue.

Before the time came to lay up, therefore, I was determined to have an engine installed in *Nightfall* while she was still at Burnham, but contrariwise I had to admit these two years of sailing her without the accompanying petrol smells and the temptation to turn the engine on at the least setback, had been very enjoyable, and strangely trouble-free. The Crouch Engineering Company, I knew, were offering a tempting line in fitting 4-cylinder Morris units, and as I sketched out the installation details at the cabin table it looked as if one of their engines would fit nicely under the existing cockpit floorboards, while . . .

"Skipper," came Nevill's voice at the helm, "there's fog coming down on this wind. You can hardly see the South Foreland now."

Seizing the little hand compass I erupted on deck, and was just in time to snatch a cross bearing of the lighthouse and the end of Dover breakwater before the clammy wreaths of fog blotted both out. The wind continued to blow steadily from the north-east, but it was damp and cold now and sent us below for jerseys and fishermen's smocks, while the mournful sound of the South Goodwin diaphone came faintly down to us on the breeze.

Soon the fog was thick around us, cutting vision to a quarter mile or so, and Marty brought out the brass fog trumpet. His lungs were in good shape, and he happily gave the regulation two blasts every so often for a sailing vessel on port tack, while *Nightfall* leant to the wind and bustled on regardless. Suddenly the hoarse voice of a steamer's whistle began to sound louder somewhere off our lee bow as she approached coming up Channel. At the same moment almost, the clearer and sharper note of a motor vessel's air syren chose to announce itself somewhere off our weather beam.

Listening carefully with that tense expectancy which comes with fog at sea, convinced that our ears were growing larger like blossoming flowers, we tried to plot the positions of the steamer and the motorship as their duet came closer. Marty with ballooned cheeks nearly blew the reed from out of the foghorn with prolonged *whoo-oo-oops* while some way off our weather bow we could now hear the mournful notes of a bell at intervals, maybe another yacht or a Thames barge. In a way we were relieved that we had no noisy engine to drown the sounds above the hiss and wash at our bow and the rhythmic crash-crash of the dinghy well astern on a long painter.

Our eyes were becoming tired through peering through the white opaqueness, convinced every so often that there in the fog was a vast black shape just about to emerge, while Marty's shattering of the quietness seemed every time to become more and more ominous. Then suddenly the steamer bellowed forth again some distance right ahead of us, and the tension eased at once as the motorship's syren roared out off our lee quarter.

"Thank God she's crossed our wake, the devil," muttered Nevill. "And that darn steamer seems to be crossing ahead of us."

The ringing of the bell was coming louder off our weather beam, and had us searching anxiously again through the fog. Marty gave another of his prolonged blasts like an injured cow, and we waited for the bell to reply.

"There she is," said Nevill, pointing astern. "Why, she's a coasting ketch."

"Could be a Manxman," suggested Marty, "with that funny round stern they used to have."

The vague shape of a deep-laden old coaster with high steeved bowsprit and the short fantail counter of the Isle of Man builders, her dark sails lifting and falling as she ran down Channel before the wind, appeared for a few moments like a ghost off our weather quarter. Then, as she crossed through our wake, she was swallowed up again in the fog, and it was difficult not to believe that she was only an apparition, a figment of our lively imagination: except that we could just hear the sound of her bell at regular intervals until it, too, faded into the distance.

As the morning advanced and we knew we were by now clear of the Channel shipping lanes, the wind began to ease off a little, and by midday the fog began to disperse in sudden patches when one could see perhaps a mile, then drifting in as dense as ever. But as we munched our cockpit lunch the sun began to break through, and all of a sudden it seemed the fog was gone, drifting away down Channel, while the sunlight began to glint on the small wavecaps.

The west-going stream had by now begun to run, and with the wind veering by degrees towards the east it was all we could do to lay up towards the Dyck light vessel. The low line of the French coast darkened the horizon beyond the lee bow, and by 1700 hours we were off the wooden piers at Gravelines, breasting a strong flood tide. For a time we discussed running into the port up its mile-long narrow channel which led to where we could make out a group of fishing boats lying on the mud in the little harbour. There would, we thought, be just enough water over the bar for our modest draught.

But on reflection it was only another 10 miles along the coast to Dunkerque, which we had had our eye on since leaving Dover, and as this breeze seemed to be holding well at east-north-east, we set our little ship at it and asked her to make as much as she could against the tide. And as the evening wore on

['The vague shape of a coaster . . .
appeared like a ghost']

the flood began to slacken, and our long and short tacking started to gain more ground on each board.

With the thought that it might be dark before we could get into Dunkerque and settle in a berth up the harbour, I wedged myself in the galley and heated up a good saucepan of stew for all hands. As the sun began to set, the breeze began freshening, and while *Nightfall* with her tiller slip-hitch held hurled herself at the short seas on the now weather-going tide, we filled ourselves with warm food and fresh vitality.

The supper dishes were washed up and stowed in their lockers by the time the piers were abeam. Soon we ran in and began a prolonged flirtation with the fickle puffs of wind coming over the windward jetty while we crept slowly up the harbour against a sluicing ebb. It was indeed after dark before we nudged ourselves into a berth where a harbour official, silhouetted on the quay against the town lights, directed us with expansive gestures and unintelligible French.

It had been our plan to push on to Ostende so as to spend a day visiting the city of Bruges, where some Belgian friends of Nevill's were living. But the tides and the winds were not favourable for making the additional 30-mile hop along the coast on the morrow. After an early breakfast we accordingly left *Nightfall* in the harbour and caught a train, to spend an interesting day with a charming family, who not only showed us some of the beautiful architectural sights of their city, but thoughtfully introduced us as well to local gastronomic pleasures. The only jarring feature of the tour was the over-powering stench which rose like a miasma from one or two of the canals in the centre of the city. Our energetic hosts appeared oblivious to the aroma, and perhaps it would be an ordinary dog's idea of heaven, but as my companions agreed in the train back to Dunkerque, it was only a matter of taste.

Early the following day we were astir with thoughts of home. The wind, we noticed, was still holding bravely in the north-east and although in the shelter of the harbour our burgee waved only listlessly, the view from the quay showed white caps racing past the pier heads. As a precaution we carefully wound two rolls in the main boom before setting sail. A purposely substantial breakfast, which included full plates of porridge as a liner for bacon and eggs, was cleared away before we cast off our lines, on the principle that it is better to put to sea with a fully belly than one that gives hollow groans at the first few heaves of the sea.

The ebbing tide carried us down the harbour with our sails once more alternately leaning over to the puffs, then hanging lifeless as the piers blanketed the channel. Outside, as expected, there was quite a good sea running with the fresh wind against a strong ebb, and, as we bore away westwards along the coast, *Nightfall* began bouncing and squirming her way over the waters. To keep the dinghy quiet we eased it astern on the end of its long painter.

It seemed to take a long time to bring the Dyck whistle buoy under our lee bow, but once we were well clear of the Snouw Bank to windward of us we were able to alter course to northwest (315° mag) for the North Goodwin light vessel.

"What about shaking out that reef?" suggested Marty after a time. "This breeze seems pretty steady."

With one accord we unrolled the boom, blessing the convenience of roller reefing, and now under plain sail (mainsail, staysail and working jib), with the wind abeam and the tide broad under her lee bow, *Nightfall* surged and dashed ahead, sailing spendidly. The asthmatic grunts and wails of the Dyck whistle buoy faded into the distance astern, and soon the low-lying land with its towers and chimneys and church spires was lost to sight.

With her 8.5m sailing waterline length *Nightfall*'s theoretical optimum speed under sail would be about 7.4 knots, and she must have been sailing close to this limit, as in the next two hours the Walker's log recorded a distance run of 14¼ miles, or an average of just over 7.1 knots through the water. The seas were not high, but a lot of them had white crests, and when one of these collided with our weather bow wave it leapt over the rail and kept our decks wet. Occasionally a steeper one than usual broke alongside the cockpit, keeping our canvas smocks wet with spray.

Steering with an arm over the tiller and one's feet against the lee coaming – *Nightfall* had an athwartship helmsman's seat – was no problem, for the little ship seemed to know where she was going and was revelling in it. But with the seas on the beam her corkscrewing motion was upsetting and tiring, and when lunchtime came round it seemed that no one was keen to volunteer to get a meal. None of us was sick – we just told each other we weren't all that hungry and would be quite happy to wait awhile, but of course if anybody wanted to go below and get himself something sustaining . . .

As the North Sand Head buoy gradually passed far away to leeward and the North Goodwin light vessel appeared broad off our weather bow, we hinted individually, then in unison, that instead of carrying on past the North Foreland and across the Estuary tonight, wouldn't it be wiser – and indeed more seamanlike, to avoid crew exhaustion – if we bore away a few degrees and pointed our wet bowsprit for Ramsgate. A night in harbour, and then we'd be full of energy for tomorrow's crossing. Besides, the south-going stream was already beginning against us at the Foreland, and hadn't we already had enough lovely sailing for one day?

Slightly salt-encrusted, and revelling in the sudden peace and warmth behind the high wall, we eased ourselves into a berth in the East Gully indicated by a harbour official, and gladly put out our fenders and lines and springs. As we looked round at the harbour with its fishing boats and trippers' craft, we congratulated ourselves on a wonderful day's sail, for we had crossed over from the piers at Dunkerque 48 miles by log to Ramsgate entrance in ten minutes over eight hours, and we promised to anoint our little ship's decks with wine.

It may have been this sense of accomplishment that reminded us that our appetites had returned in force like a nestful of baby starlings. The Customs officer came aboard and, hearing of our rapid passage, wasted no time in clearing us, and when he had departed we also lost no time in clearing up, changing into shore clothes, and tramping into the town in search of what the crew called a *properly* cooked meal.

The next morning we waited until 1000 hours for the North going tide to set in before getting underway for the Burnham river. Expecting the wind to be still in the north-east, we could scarcely believe our luck to find on getting away that the breeze was coming straight into the harbour, and we had to make two short boards to clear the south pier head. Then in sunshine and with a fast running tide in our favour we set course a little west of north for the East Margate buoy, and then north-westerly for the South Edinburgh channel.

With alternating periods of faltering, then piping up again to a welcome whole sail breeze, our passage to the Black Deep and through the Barrow Swatch into the Swin was uneventful, but as a passage under sail highly gratifying to crew and skipper. By sunset of a beautiful evening *Nightfall* was at anchor for the last night of her cruise in the Roach, and next morning she was back on her mooring off Burnham.

And not long after, well before the time came to lay up for the winter at Maldon, the little ship passed through the anchorage proudly showing how handy she could be with her newly installed Morris motor, and how from now on she and her Skipper could snap their fingers at prolonged calms.

– 4 –
Channel blows

Bound down Channel from Dover Strait on his way to the Isle of Wight, a distance of something like a hundred and ten nautical miles, the skipper of a little yacht can well be forgiven for cursing the lack of natural anchorage to offer shelter on the way. If the weather turns nasty from the south, and he and his little ship have gone too far to turn tail and run back to Dover, he has nothing but man-made harbours to offer him security.

Provided the wind is not much south of west he might be able to drop his anchor to the eastward of the prominent shingle-head of Dungeness, and here find a restless kind of shelter. To turn in to Rye Bay, on the other side of the Ness, would take him a long way out of his course, and Rye is no place for the stranger to run for if the wind comes strong from south-west, even if the tide is approaching high water. Too many craft have come to grief running for shelter into this narrow entrance with the seas breaking across.

The next port westward he could make for would be New-haven, some forty-two miles farther on, on the other side of Beachy Head. Hastings in between is but an open anchorage with only a reef of rocks giving the shore a slight lee during westerly gales, and no place for a weatherbound yacht to lie. Even the local fishing craft, the Hastings luggers and shrimpers, haul out after each trip with beach capstans. Inside the piers of Newhaven a safe berth might be obtainable in the yacht marina on the port hand, or, if our voyager objects to marina berths, he might be directed farther up the harbour to lie alongside some other craft.

Another ten miles along the coast would bring him to the big yacht marina at Brighton, with its protecting arms and safe berths, together with all sorts of local delights which can be enjoyed at a price. Since Prinny's day there has never been a place quite like Brighton. Shoreham is not much farther on, perhaps six miles, but this is another man made harbour which with Southwick and its great power station can offer the visitor a temporary berth needing the usual lines and fenders and port charges.

Farther westward still, a dozen miles or so, the long arms of Littlehampton Harbour stretch a narrow welcome into the sea. If our mariner chooses to run for it here he should be able to find at least a mud berth in the River Arun, which with all its inconveniences might be preferable to a rough night at sea. Here, too, excellent facilities are offered by local boatyards and yacht chandlers. By now, in fact, the westward-bound venturer has run out of sheltering harbours, and he must sail on round Selsey Bill and head for the bar guarding Chichester Harbour, or turn up Spithead before he will find another sheltered berth.

It would be little consolation to the skipper weary of beating up or down Channel to be told that centuries ago he would have found a number of tidal inlets and lagoons indented into this very stretch of coastline, which were deep enough for small trading vessels to run into for shelter or to unload their cargoes. It would be like assuring the traveller arriving breathless at the railway station that the local service was quite excellent, but that the last train had just gone.

Nevertheless, it is pleasant, if idle, to reflect that during the Roman Occupation, which ended around the fourth century AD, an expanse of creeks lay just west of *Portus Lemanis,* the present Hythe, where coasters could berth at quays. During the following centuries the sand and shingle banks which protected this area from the sea gradually grew outwards to form the jutting ridges of the Dungeness we know today, while the whole of the navigable creeks inland were reclaimed to become the Romney marshes.

Just east of Beachy Head, some thirty miles farther west, another extensive lagoon offered anchorage for small ships under the protection of a Roman stronghold called *Anderida* where vessels could unload at the quays. All this also became silted up, the land was reclaimed for farms, and nothing today is left to mark the area except the little river – a modest stream – that flows through Pevensey Sluice. And yet again, just to tantalise us yachtsmen, to the eastward of Selsey Bill the shallow marshy lagoon which simpers under the grandiloquent description Pagham Harbour, where only wildfowl and an occasional punt might be seen, was once an extensive inlet deep enough for coasting vessels. But Pagham Harbour is no longer of any use to a storm-tossed little ship sailor.

It could be said, therefore, that this eastern part of the English Channel can be a very exposed and uncomfortable area for small ships in any strong winds from north-east round by south to west-nor'west, with little shelter except tied up in a few artificial harbours. Perhaps my own experiences in the Channel have been responsible for a certain distrust of this whole area. For example, my first contact with the Channel was when, as a little boy, I was taken by my parents with my elder brother on one of father's annual holiday cruises from St Katharine Dock in London, round the south coast to Glasgow, and return, by one of the Clyde Shipping Company's small steamers. This was the kind of unhurried travel, with a variety of freights and a handful of passengers, which is no longer to be obtained: two weeks of shipboard life with two or three ports of call on the way, good, substantial – even to a boy's standards – Scottish cooking, and fascinating views of the English, Irish and western coastlines in turn for most of the way.

From rounding the South Foreland our tall funnelled SS

Saltees, 1100 gross tons, stuffed her bows into a strong south-westerly gale. Earliest recollections, before seasickness rendered us less appreciative, were the unbelievably huge dark green seas which hurled themselves at our aggressive bows, covering them in blinding spray, and the agonised shaking of the little vessel every time she drove into them and her screw raced. On this trip our kindly Scots captain took the steamer inside the Wight and down the Solent, so as to give his wan passengers a breathing space to recover their spirits – and we were able to gape at the upturned hull of the cruiser HMS *Gladiator*, looking like a stranded whale on the beach near Yarmouth, after her collision in the Solent in fog with the American liner *St Paul*.

At the Needles the gale met us again in all its fury, and our steamer continued once again to lift and plunge over the rushing walls of water, shaking herself and shuddering all the way to Plymouth, our first port of call where we docked over a day behind schedule. The Captain predicted no immediate let up in the stormy weather, and so together with one or two other passengers the Griffiths quartet, pale of face, empty and staggering, left the ship to return to London by train. And for years afterward little Maurice imagined the sea was always like that, for was it not confirmed by that pair of mid-Victorian engravings hanging in the hall at home, entitled *The Storm* and *The Shipwreck*?

The next occasion when I had an opportunity to try my luck with the Channel was almost twenty years later, the event the third Fastnet Race. Conor O'Brien had recently completed his voyage across three oceans and home by way of Cape Horn in his *Saoirse* and, conceivably carried away by Irish enthusiasm, had entered her for the race. *Saoirse* (Erse for 'Freedom' and pronounced, so he assured us, 'Seershay') was a small brigantine-rigged version of an Irish coaster, 42 feet on deck and built at Conor's home port of Baltimore, County Cork. With her squat hull, big stern with quarter deck and taffrails, knee high bulwarks and sharply steeved bowsprit she was, as he

['A steamer . . . driving her way
steadily down Channel]

declared, "just fine for running the Easting down", but not for
threshing to windward.

That summer of 1927 was one of the most notorious in living
memory for its succession of westerly gales, floods, thunder-
storms and wild weather generally. An account of this race has
already appeared in one of my books (*Swatchways and Little
Ships*) and need not be repeated here, but let it suffice that of the
fifteen yachts of from 12 to 30 tons Thames Measurement that
started from Cowes only two managed to fight their way round
the 625 mile course to finish at Plymouth: *La Goleta* schooner 30
tons, and *Tally Ho* gaff cutter 29 tons, the winner. Under close
reefs, *Saoirse* beat doggedly against winds reported as varying
from Force 7 to Force 9, her decks full most of the time, until
after fifty-six hours of such misery we discovered ourselves only
a little way westward of Portland Bill, making to windward no
better than a Spanish galleon.

Joy in sailing returned to us when, with unanimous acclaim, Conor put our stern to the seas and, with square fores'l and gunter mizzen pulling like horses, *Saoirse* ran back to the Needles. The sun had broken through the cloud wrack, and as we lifted our stern to a sea the scene around us looked to me like a countryside of moving green hills, their backs rolling away from us and covered in a tracery of foam that flashed in the sunlight: a beautiful and inspiring sight, so long as these hills were going our way! And the sight of a three island tramp steamer passing us half a mile off our starboard beam, as she drove her bows into the gale with the water cascading off her rusty sides and crashing against her wheelhouse windows, recalled memories of the *Saltees,* and made me appreciate that 'A life on the ocean wave, A home on the rolling deep', as the Victorian song described it, was a tough one for the professional sailor, and even in these days never without its dangers.

Bitten, perhaps, by the desire for blue water cruising as a change from our East Coast rivers and creeks, my partner and I planned to use our fortnight's summer holiday the following year in a cruise down Channel and back in my 8-tonner *Wilful*, a sturdy flush-decked 30ft cutter with a deep draught, built by Sibbick at Cowes in 1899. Crossing the Thames Estuary before a flukey north-east breeze, we looked forward to an easy run down Channel. But Aeolus must have noticed us as we cleared the Downs, and smiled to himself; for as we opened the South Foreland and saw the waters of the Channel before us, the wind flew into the south-west and the barometer started to drop fast.

Despite these depressing signs of harsher weather to come, we hardened our hearts against the temptation to put into Dover and wait for a slant, and carried on close-hauled, making long boards towards the French coast and back, tacking at the change of each four hour watch. The plunging and slicing into every sea was mild purgatory, for with her lean bow sections and deep lead keel *Wilful*'s motion always contrived to make me sick when at sea, while it even overcame the Mate's normally immune stomach.

Sometime during the second night the wind strengthened in earnest and reached what we logged as gale force. We managed to stuff three more rolls in the mainsail and threshed on with storm jib, until as dawn began to break we could make out the piers of Newhaven, and by common consent scuttled into blessed peace of the harbour, while a full south-westerly gale sent its swell rolling up the harbour as we lay alongside a laden barge, weather-bound like ourselves, with our fenders squeaking and springs jerking. The full story of this checkered cruise – which ended with days of fitful airs, maddening calms and a glassy sea – appeared in *The Magic of the Swatchways*, but I have mentioned it here just to show how one's early experiences can colour one's impressions.

A further reflection could be made on our very unwise decision to ignore the barometer and sky signs off Dover and to plug on against a rising south-wester. Soft and tired from exacting shore jobs, now wet, cold and approaching complete exhaustion, we were only one step from getting ourselves into serious difficulties. During that second night out, had *Wilful*'s mainsail, for example, split across (as it did in another gale later that season), or the peak halyards parted, or a seam opened up in the garboards and started a serious leak, we would have been in no condition to deal with any such emergency in any forceful and adequate way. We lacked the experience – indeed, the common sense – to realise what we were taking on with the weather evidently deteriorating, and our foolhardiness followed by the effects of seasickness and sheer physical exhaustion could quickly have led us into the familiar situation where flares have to be used to call the Lifeboat. It is said that we live and learn, but I have done many silly things in boats since then, and I sometimes wonder how many of us really profit by our mistakes?

It was some years after this before I returned to do battle with the waters of the English Channel. This time it was as an invited crew aboard a Class II competitor in the Royal Ocean Racing Club's race from Cowes to Dinard. The yacht was of a traditional slender racing type with overhanging bow and long thin counter, the product of a clever designer whose yachts were noted for their ability to win cups. To achieve these results the scantlings – the main constructional members of the hull – were cut down to the limit so as to save as much weight as possible, and it was not surprising, therefore, that some of these boats had a reputation for being not only very wet on deck, but also for working when driven hard into a head sea. It is not difficult to imagine that when a wooden yacht with a long overhanging bow pounds into the face of a steep sea, the tall mast with all its sails and rigging snatches at the bar-taut shrouds, which put huge strains on the chainplates attached to the topsides. In addition, the concentrated weight of the lead keel hanging down beneath the garboards at an angle as she heels, wrenches at the athwartship frames or floors, putting severe wringing stresses below the waterline. The whole structure of the hull tends to warp and flex under the constantly varying strains of waves and weight and wind pressure on the sails, and in hard weather conditions the seams of a wooden hull naturally tend to work and let in the water.

It was blowing a stiff breeze from south-west as the fleet began to work their way round Bembridge Ledge and stretched out close-hauled away from the lee of the Wight. As one by one the yachts disappeared behind a driving mist and the wind piped up to a moderate gale, the conditions reminded me forcibly of that earlier race with Conor O'Brien. But at any rate, this yacht was no lurching, full-bodied Irish brigantine, but a long and sleek racing sloop with many challenge cups to her record.

With only one reef in our mainsail and the No 1 jib pulling her like a dray horse, our yacht was clearly overpressed and dipping her lee rail well under water. But with her long overhangs at bow and stern and comparatively low freeboard, she rated badly in her class, and our Skipper was understandably determined to drive her for all she was worth, to get up in front and darn well stay there. He accordingly kept her at it, driving her long snout into the great breaking seas while she pounded at times as though she had hit a concrete wall.

Below decks the noise forward was deafening, the saloon as moist as a Turkish bath, and all the berths were already sopping wet. As the seas broke on board and washed along the weather deck I had never before seen water squirting in such quantities through the entire length of the carline, while every so often it gushed down between the mast wedges as if from a hosepipe.

As darkness began to close over the wild scene like a clammy hand, the bilge water began to wash over the lee side of the cabin floorboards and surge up the side of the hull, where it struck the underside of the deck and washed back onto the watch below in their lee berths. Muffled curses could be heard coming from beneath the sodden blankets, but in time even these human sounds gave way to silence as seasickness took its toll. On deck, in the exposed position of the long shallow cockpit, the crew on watch ducked every few seconds to dodge the cold driving spray, with expressions beneath their oilies that suggested something less than enthusiasm.

Blest with an iron stomach, or perhaps driven by an inner anxiety, our Skipper nobly crawled forward into the forepeak with a torch, where he crouched peering in the rays of the lamp into the long dark tunnel of the yacht's bow. Twice, as she dropped her snout over a crest into the trought beyond, he was lifted off hands and knees and cracked his head on a convenient deck beam. But not once did he raise his voice in blasphemy, for he was a religious man. What he did discover, however, brought him back stern first with a melancholy expression. Those of us in the watch below shook the water out of our ears to hear what he had to say.

"She's opened up one of the seams in the bow," he told us. "In fact it's running in pretty fast when she pounds and the seam works. We'll have to keep pumping."

And pump we did, while the other hands fought the sodden folds of the mainsail and tied down the third reef and set the No 3 jib. While the seas rolling up Channel steadily grew higher and more menacing, our game little vessel seemed easier and no longer leapt so far beyond the breaking crests to land with such mast-shaking crashes beyond. But as fast as the neat little yacht type bilge pump chucked out the water, so it continued to pour in through a dozen places in hull and decks, and the lee side of the saloon was still being washed like an overhanging cliff in an onshore gale. If there was any dry and comfortable spot below that night, it completely eluded us.

Our navigator reckoned we were now about sixty miles on our way across Channel (not quite one third of the race course) and still hopefully up with the leaders of our class, although in the darkness and spray we could catch no glimpse of any of the other competitors. But the crew's stamina was beginning to flag, while as fast as we managed to pump the bilges dry the water was washing over the lee berths again, and there is nothing quite like a constant leak which could become worse at any moment to lower the morale of a ship's company. After studying the chart and a short confab with those on deck, the Skipper sadly decided enough was enough, and gave the order to abandon the race and bear away for home.

"And to think," he remarked mournfully, while the slamming of the bows gave way to the exhilarating lift and scend before the quartering seas as we started our run back to the shelter of the Isle of Wight, "to think how much it costs just to *do* this! Whatever gave me the ocean racing bug, I'll never know."

I've often wondered.

– 5 –
Who would
a-racing go?

The way the racing yachtsman approaches his sport is very different from that of the average cruising man. The dedicated racing man who is worth his salt goes all out for efficiency in his boat, in her gear and equipment, and in his crew; and when not in a race what sailing the crew do together is usually taken up in sail-changing practice, spinnaker drill, tacking, gybing and every type of race manoeuvre, so that they will become a highly effective team.

The dyed-in-the-wool cruising man, on the other hand, is generally worlds away from such tense efficiency. So long as his boat sails well enough, and the leech of the mainsail or jib doesn't keep flogging all the time when close-hauled, he'll be quite content to sit at his tiller and sail peacefully to whatever anchorage he has in mind for the night. But let him ship a keen racing man to crew him one weekend and he'll be astonished at the number of things that will be wrong with his boat.

"Skipper," the eager hand will murmur, "the mains'l's setting like a sack. Let me take up a bit on that leechline. And the foot needs a bit more hauling out at the clew: it'll take all those wrinkles out."

The owner will have to admit the sail does set better now, while his nimble crew catches hold of the jibsheet and, peering up at the leech, tries varying the angle of its lead.

"The jib fairlead wants to be moved a couple of inches farther inboard," he says. "And about six inches aft, don't you think?"

With the crew's foot holding the sheet down on deck at the suggested position the owner has to admit to himself that the jib really does set better now. Maybe he *should* move that sheet lead.

"Another thing." His crew won't let him sit back and rest yet. "I get the impression she'll go better if we trim her an inch or two down at the bow. I notice she's dragging a bit too much of her transom, and that slows her. You've got some ballast inside which we could move, haven't you?"

With an idea as to who will actually move the pigs of rusty ballast, the owner sighs at the lack of rest with a keen racing type aboard. But when the alterations have all been done and he has cleaned his bandaged fingers, the owner does have to admit that his old boat is going better than she did before, and he ought to admit some gratitude to his friend's keenness.

An old yachting friend of mine was an unusual combination for a dedicated yachtsman, for he not only loved cruising and during his lifetime owned a series of true cruising boats from a small oyster smack to a sturdy 35ft ketch of 15 tons TM; but he was also a superb helmsman, and a consistent winner in local One-Design racing, in the old 8-Metre cruiser-racer class, and in International Dragons. He used to sail with me now and again and taught me innumerable wrinkles about getting a boat along through the water. In his own river, knowing all the tide changes and eddies, he was almost unbeatable, and with his quick eye he often pointed out how to look for their signs on the surface.

Aboard my own boat he would spend a lot of time adjusting parts of the mainsail until there was not a wrinkle anywhere on its surface (details I was ashamed to say I had never bothered about), sheets would be eased or hardened an inch at a time and the set of the headsails corrected. And when he had finished to his satisfaction I had to admit that in light winds at least my ship did go a little faster, and she appeared to like it.

While we were lying at anchor in the Crouch one year watching the racing during Burnham Week, it was a revelation to me to hear him discuss the finer points of the various classes of yachts as they passed, details that I would have missed: the reason why such and such a boat was now drawing ahead; why that laggard was well behind because the helmsman wouldn't keep his tiller still; the badly set genoa here, the mainsheet there a little – an inch or two – too tight in; a crew hand sitting in the wrong position to trim the boat, a helmsman there steering throughtlessly so that in a few minutes his boat would be feeling a foul wind from another boat ahead, and so on.

It was with the conviction that there was far more to know about tuning a yacht and racing her than met the eye (I had already absorbed as much as I understood of Manfred Curry's thought-provoking book, *Yacht Racing: Aerodynamics of Sail*) that I decided to volunteer to crew in one of the handicap races if the opportunity arose. While the *Yachting Monthly* was essentially a cruising yachtman's magazine, I felt that whatever its editor could learn from the racing fraternity would be all to the good.

The chance of such an experience came sooner than expected. Jack Laurent Giles had designed for a client what was described as a cruising 8-Metre, an advanced design for that date (1934), and he had sailed her round from Lymington to take part in the Royal Corinthian Yacht Club's Estuary Race. The owner was unable to accompany her for this overnight event and Jack was put in charge.

Étain was a sleek beauty with the long overhangs of the contemporary 'Eights', 46ft overall with 9ft beam and 6.6ft draught and rigged as what was then commonly called a slutter, namely a Bermudian two-headsail sloop or stemhead cutter – make your own choice. Jack needed another hand to make up his complement of five, and invited me to join them. With the designer himself as skipper who would be sure to get the best out of his own offspring, and in such an outstanding type of yacht, it was an opportunity not to be missed.

It could not have been without a sense of humour that Jack had selected the members of his crew. Except for John, who as *Étain*'s regular crew was to prove an admirable hand in every way, the three of us volunteers were owners of tough cruising boats, and none of us had become a convert to an 8-Metre for fast cruising – as yet. For myself, I could not wait to see what a yacht of *Étain*'s thoroughbred type could do in our Estuary seas, and hoped there would be plenty of wind for the race.

There was. Before the start the barometer had dropped three tenths in as many hours, and the day of the equinox gave us all a fine experience of appropriate weather. Our course was to take us from the start off Burnham round the Longsand Head buoy and the Kentish Knock light vessel, past the Tongue light vessel, up the narrow Princes Channel to the Girdler light vessel, then through the sands to the South Oaze buoy, down Swin to the Whitaker Spit buoy and back to Burnham – ninety uneasy miles. It was evidently going to be a hard and wet race, for the third year in succession.

Our most serious competitor was going to be *Rosemary V*, a fine 40ft (12 metre) racing sloop designed by Alfred Mylne, and we watched her carefully. The remainder of the twelve starters did not bother us much as they were mostly an unexciting lot which included several old gaff cutters and a fifty-year-old ex-Colchester smack named *Dusmarie*. With a stiff breeze blowing from the south-south-west and a light driving rain the fleet foamed down the Crouch with the older cutters dragging themselves under topsails.

Down the Whitaker and out into the East Swin we drove, with the whole mainsail and high-clewed No1 jib pressing our slender 46-footer as much as she would take. The speedometer was holding its needle at a steady 8 knots, and during one vicious squall it rose to 8½. This was exhilarating sailing but too hard on the yacht and her gear, and soon Jack had us scrambling forward along her side deck. The jib was sent down, unhanked and bundled onto the floor of the saloon, a sodden mound of creamy canvas. Working thus it was 'one hand for

['With a stiff breeze blowing . . . and a
light driving rain']

the ship, t'other for yourself' on the steeply slanting decks, for
there were no pulpits, guard rails or lifelines aboard these
yachts as yet, and working hands had to mind the age-old rules
of seamen at sea.

Already we had worked out a lead of a quarter of a mile from
the front-runners of the fleet, and hoped to hold it. The Gunfleet pile lighthouse passed away to leeward, and before the
heavier rain came we could discern the distant shoreline of the
Naze and Harwich Harbour. Then a heavier squall than before
blotted out the land and *Étain* buried her lee deck once again.
The skipper looked up at her lofty mast whipping against the
grey sky.

"We must get a reef in, you fellows."

It seemed a shame to have to throw away our fine lead from those other yachts, hurrying after us like hounds after a fox. But *Étain* was crying out for relief, and with the No 2 jib aback she lay quietly hove-to while we struggled with the leech tackle and reef points, gripping the wet skylight with our knees and toes, while inexorably one yacht in the fleet after another caught up and swept by, with the spume from their bow waves blowing away to leeward like steam.

Far away through the rain we could see two of the yachts apparently running down wind towards Harwich, while the old smack appeared to be doggedly coming along, but with her topsail now sent down and her mainsail well triced up. If she was like the old smack I had owned a few years before, I grinned inwardly at the thought, she would be like a half tide rock in these short seas when she came on the wind at the Longsand Head turning mark.

As we hauled our sheets the squalls came fast and furious, and it soon became clear that *Étain* would be overpressed on the wind without a second reef in her big mainsail. Once again we hove-to with jib aback and allowed our ship to look after herself, which she did very comfortably, while we fought hard wet canvas and elusive reef pendants, and the Longsand Head buoy rose and fell and reeled away to windward of us.

"I didn't think this type of boat would lie quiet like this," someone remarked above the shriek of the wind, and our Skipper laughed.

"You'll see a lot of what she can do yet," he said, shaking the water from his oilskins. "Come on, get that luff really taut, boys."

Once more *Étain* heeled over and, close-hauled now on starboard tack, drove her fine bow at the racing seas. *Blue Jay*, the pretty 39ft yawl of Albert Strange design had stowed her large jib at last, and was bucking along to leeward under the press of her four lowers; *Cooya*, a slightly larger yawl by Linton Hope, had finished reefing her mainsail and was underway again half a mile astern, while to our astonished satisfaction *Rosemary*, our chief rival, had disappeared into the murk to leeward with the remainder of the fleet in the direction of the Suffolk coast.

"Good lord, look there!"

Jack was pointing away to *windward*, and there we could discern a small white square-sterned cutter plunging into it as gamely as you please. She was *Sunshine*, an 8-tonner only 27½ft in length, whose skipper had wisely reefed while well to windward of the turning mark and had come running down towards us while we were struggling with our own reef points. We'd certainly have to show a clean pair of heels in the form of our long and pointed counter before the day was much older, we told ourselves, if our reputation as a fast 8-Metre wasn't to be blown away with the wind. Little transom-sterned cutter, of all things!

The spring ebb was racing away towards the north-east at three knots or more and with our course reckoned 185° magnetic for the next mark, the Kentish Knock, and the wind hardly anything west of 205°, our actual course over the ground on the starboard tack must have been leading us well out towards theBelgian coast. It was blowing more fiercely than ever now and raining harder, and soon visibility must have been well under half a mile. The barometer was still falling, and as we crashed into the angry seas, pausing on the crest before dropping with a shudder into the trough, *Étain* began to flood her whole lee deck and started to labour once more.

We were dropping little *Sunshine* astern gradually, for she was not able to point quite so high as this sleek racer. Slowly she passed away from our weather quarter to dead astern, and then to our lee quarter, until finally the gathering murk enveloped her and we saw her no more that night. When the four brown sails of the yawl *Blue Jay*, which was still away on our port beam but sagging farther and farther to leeward, were also swallowed up, we suddenly realised that the last of our competitors had disappeared from view, and the sea became lonelier, more cold and more dreary than before.

Étain shovelled her long snout out of a crest, fell in a sweeping arc and crashed into the heart of a towering monster of a wave. A bore of water surged aft along the weather deck, gushed over into the cockpit, cascaded through the half open doors on to the heap of sodden sails piled over the companion steps, and trickled through the skylight. The seas were growing heavier, and with too much canvas aloft *Étain* was punishing herself with an abandoned frenzy.

"Third reef, chaps! Lively now."

It was with almost a feeling of relief that we scrambled on deck and tackled that third and last reef, even though John had to balance on the after deck to reach the swaying boom-end so as to re-reeve the leech tackle. This deep reef had only eyelets in the sail instead of hanging reef pendants, and the end of the lacing had to be taken under the boom and rove through each eyelet in turn.

Soaked to the skin, we dragged the canvas down, struggled, slipped, swore and laughed, and as the greyness of the evening turned imperceptibly to an ominous gloom of a dirty night, our game little ship plunged on again, close-reefed but decidedly more comfortable. While the main hatch was open one of us fell on to the heap of wet sails below, cursing loudly.

Jack looked up from the chart he was pouring over, and grinned. "Take it easy," he chuckled, "worse things happen at sea!"

For a time the yacht seemed to behave more serenely, with less violent dives and not so many heavy thuds on her weather bow. Jack clambered into the cockpit to the helmsman.

"What are we doing?" he asked, glancing at the speedo-meter.

"$5\frac{1}{2}$, Skipper."

"Not enough. You're sailing her too fine. Give it her full."

The needle rose. 6 knots. $6\frac{1}{2}$. 7.

"That's fine. Keep her at it like that. Ease her only over the biggest ones."

For part of my watch on deck I sat enthralled in the corner of

the self-draining cockpit. 7 knots close-hauled through such sea
on a 31ft waterline. I had never sailed so fast to windward
before in so small a ship. No longer were we going easily, as no
doubt I should have sailed her had I been cruising instead of
racing; the bows banged into the seas and drove sheets of spray
high in the air, to fall in crashes on the bottom of the upturned
dinghy, and over the heads and shoulders of those of us in the
cockpit.

Below once again in the saloon, where the lamps had already
been lighted, I found Jack once more studying the sodden
Estuary chart, dripping but clearly happy, and Watkins
wedged up on the lee settee. He grinned.

"She's an eye-opener," he said, "isn't she?" He was himself
the owner of a sturdy 36ft gaff cutter, *White Heather*, which had
just won the RORC Channel race in somewhat similar nasty
weather that summer. Sitting there on the wet sails, soaked and
shivering, yet astonished at the comparative quiet, even the
relatively easy motion, below decks, I agreed she certainly was
a remarkably fast and able boat and a wizard at fetching to
windward.

"Hold tight, chaps!"

At the helmsman's shout, echoless and distant as a cry in the
night, we held on and felt *Étain* reel as her bow lifted to a dizzy
height, hovered, and then fell with a deafening crash and a
jarring of crockery in the galley. John's cheery face beamed in
the doorway, followed by what seemed a flood of water.

"That was a big one, sir," he said, grinning.

So it went on, while the night became black as the inside of a
chimney stack and the wind increasing with the darkness drove
rain and spray at us and, with consistent cruelty, veered more
round to the west, in our very teeth. Not a light was to be seen
anywhere, not even a glimmer from the Kentish Knock, our
next turning mark, and we wondered just how far to the eastward that sluicing spring ebb had set us. How soon dare we go
in on the port tack without fetching up on the Knock sands?
And just how far astern of us were those two game rivals with

their good handicaps, *Blue Jay* and the little *Sunshine*? And whereabouts was our chief rival, *Rosemary V*?

It was a colourless prospect, that vile night, and the utter blackness didn't help the Skipper in his courageous decision to keep her at it, come what may. In the ordinary way of good seamanship when cruising it had become time to heave-to and wait for better visibility and a sight of some recognisable light. But Jack knew his *Étain*.

"She'll stand any amount of driving," he said cheerfully, the only one of the ship's company with John not to be sick by then. "We've got to keep her going. She's not dependent on a twelve-foot bowsprit, you know."

And keep her crashing into it we did, while the tide turned and with the weather-going flood the seas began to tumble over in frothy flashes of white, like flurries of snow in the darkness. It was a long night, and it seemed to become colder. Wet to the skin and still retching at regular intervals, I was finding even the two-hour tricks at the helm trying, although I had to admit *Étain* was a revelation to steer. Under her reduced sail area she felt beautifully balanced, needing only a little weather helm even when heeled to the covering board, enabling the helmsman to hold her with only one hand, while the other could gain some warmth and feeling in his oilskin pocket.

She was eager and immediately responsive, and when a higher crest than usual loomed out of the night, he had only to ease the helm down a few inches to bring her almost head-on to the wave. Then sharply up with the helm again as her bow sliced through the crest, to crash down into the trough beyond and ready, full-and-bye, to take on the next. But this cold was growing more and more penetrating, and at the end of the two-hour trick it was a relief to slip below into the comparative peace and warmth of the saloon, and subside on to the folds of the big jib and reach for one's comfort bowl! No doubt we all catnapped, for despite the all-pervading aura of damp and discomfort, there were jokes and laughter, and had a sepulchral voice come from the darkness outside "Why do you fellows *choose* to go yachting on a night like this?" I don't think we should have been lost for an answer.

The first light that was sighted around midnight was – the South Foreland! It was away off our port bow and yellow with distance. We were miles and miles to the eastward of our course. Then the rain suddenly cleared and the bright North Foreland flashed out, closer aboard, but still far ahead. And ahead of us, too, lay some thirty miles of wind-racked Thames Estuary for us to work through to the Tongue light vessel, our next mark, with the hard wind blowing into our teeth. It was for me at least a prospect to cause another bout of shivering!

The sky began to clear in rifts, and a full moon of a metallic brightness lit up the heaving waters and revealed us, a ghostly tall pyramid of white, smashing and leaping over the dark growling seas. The clouds dispersed, driving across the sky and revealing the stars in their groups, and the cold light of the moon, plunging through isolated wind-blown clouds as if they were smoke, lit up the horizon and showed clearly the white upperworks of big ships; while behind the lights of a trawler as she swept by her rigging appeared etched against the horizon.

Blowing every bit as strongly as ever, now from the west, the wind had headed us again. All night long we made dogged tacks up the tortuous, buoy-infested Princes Channel, dodging one steamer after another. Our sidelights would not have kept alight for more than a few minutes through all this wind and shaking, and a torch was accordingly kept to hand by the helmsman to flash on the sails if necessary; but in brilliant moonlight like this and with a good lookout it was never needed. It is as well, however, that offshore racing rules concerning navigation lights have long since been tightened up. Maybe we were just pioneers and didn't know it.

Our fair flood ran itself out as we continued to beat, and the next ebb, fierce as any Solent tide, turned in our teeth and made those weary miles past the Shingles and the Pan Sand and the Girdler a prolonged misery of soaked clothes and cutting, icy wind. The dashes of spray felt warm and comforting in comparison! American tourists might have described it as typical English summer weather.

The sky paled in the east and the first rays of the sun, yellow and hard-looking, stretched across the sawtooth horizon as we beat past the Girdler and the Shivering Sand. It was almost dead low water by now, and the sands would be showing their smoother backs when the sun rose. A steamer coming down out of the Thames forced us about to leeward of our next mark, the South Oaze buoy, and we unknowingly carried on too long on the starboard tack. Heeling to our covering board and still sailing hard, we fit the sand with a sudden shock; paused, lifted and hit again with a vicious tautening of the rigging.

Étain came to a stop and lay still, heeled to her rail, in about four feet of water, while we swore severally and in unison. It looked as though all chances of doing anything creditable in this race were now blown away with the wind.

To windward of us, as the light grew stronger with the first tip of the sun over the horizon, we could discern the waves breaking on the shoal and a flat stretch of yellow sand between them and ourselves. That was why we were so comparatively still. The chart told us we had just caught the eastern tail of the Red Sand, and with whatever patience we still possessed we just had to settle down and wait for the tide to make about three feet.

With his binoculars our Skipper scanned the horizon carefully for a sight of any of our competitors. Nothing but steamers, a motor barge and a Thames barge with her topsail lowered to the cap could be seen. Our hopes began to return, while I for one secretly felt the fates had been kind to offer this opportunity for an hour or two's rest from all the turmoil.

"Just in time to get some eggs and bacon for breakfast," I said. "I'll cook it. How many eggs everybody?"

The others, unaccustomed to so frequent an occurrence in this Thames Estuary, looked at me as though I were demented.

"We'd better launch the dinghy," said Jack, "and layout the kedge first."

"Without appearing to be a rebellious crew, Jack," I told him, "I don't think there's any need to do that. If we just leave one of the headsails up we'll blow off in under two hours and be on our way again."

Somewhat reluctantly the Skipper acquiesced while I rigged up the stove to suit the yacht's angle. But she was at least steady and we all had a good breakfast, which filled our aching insides and put warmth and new life into us, while we also changed from some of our sodden clothes. It felt wonderful, and when the water made a few feet and *Étain*, bless her stout heart, came upright and with only one or two teeth-jarring bumps started sailing again, it was still only eight o'clock. A tug which had steamed as close as she dare and had waited near the edge of the shoal scenting salvage of a 'proper gen'leman's little yacht', belched a black cloud of smoke from her funnel and turned away with an air of disgust.

The run down Swin against the strong flood was comparatively slow, even though we had set a jib tops'l to the masthead, but we were wise to resist the temptation to shake out those reefs from the mainsail, for on that tedious 14-mile beat from the Whitaker Spit buoy up the long narrow channel into the Crouch the wind blew more strongly than ever, and continued to hurl mean little dashes of cold spray at us. My casual cruising instinct suggested that there seemed little point now to continue to sail and handle the headsheets as though our lives depended on it, and, left alone, I should have made a less strenuous job of these hundreds of short tacks. Wisely I kept my mouth shut, for once.

But Jack, the racing skipper, was quite right in not letting up until we were over the finishing line off the Royal Corinthian.

"Keep at it, chaps," he advised. "We'll make as good a show as we can to the finish."

After picking up a mooring we searched with salt-encrusted eyes for earlier arrivals. A boatman came off and told us we were the first boat in. We gaped at him. But what of all our sturdy rivals, the quay punt, the out-and-out sea-keeping cruisers, the yachts that were built for just such weather as we'd had? Where had they got to while we had been set miles miles to leeward of the Kentish Knock and rested for nearly two hours on the Red Sand? We again gazed sleepily round the crowded anchorage.

None had come in, he told us. Eight, he'd learnt, had run into Harwich, two – *Blue Jay* and the game little *Sunshine* – were at Ramsgate, and one other boat had perhaps wisely returned to her moorings here at Burnham. We had apparently sailed round the course alone.

"D'you mean – we've won?" we asked incredulously.

The boatman pushed off with a sweeping glance over our sleek decks.

"Course you have sir. So you should've with a blooming racing yacht like that!"

[Jack heron]

– 6 –
Just a
helping hand

For the past few days sailing conditions had been all one could hope for during a spell of anti-cyclonic weather in mid-summer. Since dropping our mooring at Pin Mill, in the Orwell, each morning a sea breeze had filled in from south-east, growing almost fresh by early afternoon, then dying away little by little to a soft and gentle air as evening wore on. And each night we had been lying in a calm in one favourite anchorage after another.

Our wandering during this idyllic week had been far from venturesome, for my crew on this occasion consisted of Bill, an old shipmate and doctor friend, tired out as he said from working too hard too long at Barts, and Young Cliff, a capable Westcountry sailor who had never before sailed in the sandy waters of the Thames Estuary, and just wanted to see some of the places he had so often read about.

After making the almost classic tour of familiar anchorages, from a night off Waldringfield in the Deben, and by way of Walton Backwaters, Pyfleet Creek, Maldon and through the Rays'n Channel, we had sailed up the Crouch for a night anchored above Fambridge in Brandyhole Reach. All crowded anchorages had been bypassed while we merely scrutinised with critical eyes the hundreds of different yachts on moorings as we sailed past.

On the Saturday, after a long day exploring the Roach and the creeks inside Havengore, we brought up close to the Foulness Island shore in the lower reach so as to be ready to take the morrow's ebb back to Pin Mill. All three had to be back at our jobs in London on Monday morning, and we were determined therefore to be back in time to catch the Sunday evening train at Ipswich.

As it was Saturday night, I reminded my excellent shipmates that all the Burnham waterside pubs would now be ablaze with lights and awash with beery laughter and noise, and wouldn't they . . . ? But neither was tempted, and declared that they were completely happy just to relax in *Nightfall*'s cabin, smoke their pipes, and talk about all the places and the boats we had been seeing these past few days. After all, there was all the food and drink we needed in the lockers, and it was very peaceful on board.

With Sunday morning a sea-change appeared to have come over the weather pattern. The bulkhead barometer, high all week, had risen even further, and on deck we found the wind had backed a little more into the east, briskly sweeping across the meadows on Foulness and rustling the marram grass on the river wall. By the time breakfast was cleared and stowed away a mist had come driving in, a sea fret, clammy and cold, paling the rays of the sun, an abrupt change from the summery conditions of the past few days.

High water had come and gone, and in the leisurely end of cruise way my companions had tended to linger over their pipes, and I was beginning to feel impatient at losing even an hour or so of a fair tide. It was with a sudden feeling of urgency therefore that the anchor was broken out and I cranked up the engine. After sailing up and down the coast over the past two seasons without a motor, my trusty 31ft gaff cutter had been fitted with a sturdy converted car engine, taken from the chassis of a bullnose Morris the previous winter. With the ebb running to the northward therefore *Nightfall* muttered her way out of the Roach and down the Crouch on the fast running tide.

The wind seemed to be increasing by degrees and the mist thickening, so that the sea walls at Shore Ends were scarcely visible on either side. Then soon all land had disappeared. But we found we could just lay down the Whitaker Channel with long and short tacks. mainsail, jib and staysail were set, and the Morris switched off.

For some time there was no sound above the singing of the wind in the rigging, the rhythmic lift and *whoosh* of the bow waves, and the fussing of the dinghy towing astern. Had it not been so long after high water I should have been tempted to bear away here and sail back through the Rays'n to the Wallet, but even with our draught of only a little over a metre I felt this channel had grown too many shoal patches over the years and at this state of tide could easily bedevil our plans. It was thought wiser therefore to press on down Whitaker to the deeper Spitway.

The fog, driving past in clammy wreaths that sent us below for our fishermen's smocks, was becoming so thick that the West Buey buoy slipped past somewhere to leeward unseen. It was not until after two short boards the South Buxey loomed up close under our lee bow, we knew exactly where we were, and I could coil down the dripping leadline for the time being.

Nightfall was beginning to rear and buck into a swell that appeared to be coming in against the ebb. It was not a violent swell, perhaps five feet from trough to crest, but a longer, entirely different kind of sea of the usual short wind-against-tide chop you get hereabouts.

"Wonder where it's coming from," remarked Cliff. "Didn't think you had such things on the East Coast."

"Capful o' wind somewhere out there in the North Sea, I shouldn't wonder," Bill said as he nursed the tiller under his arm. "Could be a nor'easterly blow, say, in the German Bight, couldn't it?"

Whatever the cause, the roar of the swell as it broke all along the edge of the Buxey to leeward was an ominous sound, and Cliff remarked what a hell of a place it would be to go ashore in thick weather like this amongst all these shoals. His Westcountry-bred soul must have yearned for the deeper clearer waters of the Channel.

From our last southward tack we had not caught a glimpse of either the Whitaker beacon or any other marks, and closing the edge of the sand where we hoped the Swin Spitway would be, we were straining our senses for sight of the buoy or sound of its bell. The lines of a ballad kept running absurdly through my head:

> *The good old Abbot of Aberbrothock*
> *Had placed the bell on the Inchcape Rock*
> (But it was Ralph the wicked Rover who had cut it adrift, and)
> *Down sank the Bell with a gurgling sound*
> *The bubbles arose and burst all around*

"I can hear it!" Cliff's keen ears were quicker than ours, and as the mournful tolling reached us the big cage buoy lurched into view, reeling and wallowing in the sandy-looking seas.

With sheets eased we swept past the clanging monster and steered on a north-north-westerly course through the swash between the sands, until we could put the Wallet Spitway buoy astern and overhaul sheets again for Harwich. We were in comparatively smooth water now, for the sands to windward of us were beginning to uncover and give us a fine lee. But the distant roar of the seas on the other side of the banks continued to remind us of the ominous swell still running in from the north.

Cliff suddenly pointed to windward. "What's that noise, out there?" he asked.

From somewhere away to seaward we could all hear it now: very faint sounds, like a donkey in pain, repeated over and over.

"Some chap a bit jittery about this fog, I'd say," suggested Bill. "Sounds a bit frantic, doesn't he." The eerie grunts continued with only short pauses, *whoop, whoop*.

"If he's over *there*," I thought aloud, pointing through our weather shrouds, "he must be right over the Gunfleet in its shallowest part."

"Poor blighter, he must be in trouble then. Oughtn't we to go looksee, skipper?"

Sheets were hardened in at once and our little ship luffed up and headed towards the edge of the sands. The sound of the foghorn was becoming clearer, right ahead now, its doleful notes more intermittent, as though the operator was running short of breath. I fetched our own trumpet out of the locker and handed it to Bill.

"Give him a toot or two," I told him, "just to let him know we've heard him."

Bill's long wail was echoed by a renewed series of *whoops* to windward. Cliff was pointing excitedly.

"Look, there he is. Fine on the bow."

Through the driving mist we could just make out the shape of a small yacht aground, her mast swaying violently from side to side as each wave ran across the sands, lifted her a moment,

['. . . to see what assistance they need.']

and dropped her bilge on the hard ground. A figure was hanging on to the shrouds with one hand and waving, but we could not hear a word of what he was shouting. It put an icy grip on the heart to see the helpless movements of the little vessel, and it reminded me sharply of a dreadful night a dozen years earlier – in the autumn of 1923 – which another friend and I spent aground on these very sands in his old centreboarder *Albatross*; and how we came very near to losing her (and very likely ourselves as well, for our dinghy had gone adrift) before we managed to get her off as dawn was breaking.

"We'll sail in as close as we can," I said as the lead hit bottom at three fathoms, "bring up, and go over in the dinghy and see what assistance they need."

Blessing once more *Nightfall*'s shallow draught, I took her in over the edge of the sands while Cliff and Bill on the foredeck sent the stays'l down and then stowed the main. Under jib we stemmed the lee-bowing tide for a time, until the lead showed us a fathom and a half, and then the jib was rolled up and the anchor let go on a sheer.

"Will you take the dinghy, Bill," I told him, "with Cliff, and row over and see what's to be done? I'll stay on board as this sand's not good holding ground."

My trusty shipmates took an oar each and rowed steadily towards the stricken yacht. The dinghy almost disappeared behind some of the steeper swells and absurdly reminded me of an old engraving which hung in a room at home, *The Launch of the Lifeboat*. The yacht, although only just discernible through the driving mist, was less than a quarter of a mile away, and it was not long before Bill and Cliff were ranging alongside her. Through the binoculars I could see that she was some kind of cutter-rigged lifeboat conversion, and that she was already ceasing to roll back and forth and gradually setting down on her port bilge.

It was half an hour or more before my friends returned. "It's a young chap with his wife and two small children," Bill explained as they clambered aboard. "I managed to calm the wife down a bit, for she was almost hysterical, but the kids are cold and wet and scared. They really are in a bit of a pickle."

"The chap seemed surprised," said Cliff, "when we told him they were on the Gunfleet. He seemed to think they'd caught the Whitaker Spit – he evidently didn't know where he was. Said they'd come from the Medway."

"They're certainly not in a nice position if this wind really pipes up, and brings in a bigger sea across those sands. I don't know how you chaps feel, but I reckon we'll just have to stand by till they float. If it blows hard their boat could break up."

"I'm glad you agree, Skipper," said Bill, "for the poor chap – his name's Ernest, by the way – begged us not to go away and leave them. Cliff has volunteered to go aboard and help them sail off, if you're agreeable. They'll need help, for the wife isn't much of a sailorman, and their boat's apparently leaking badly after the bumping they've had and Ernest could do with another hand at the pump."

Before long the sands were bare, and only the continuous roar of the seas on the other side of them remained to remind us of the anger that was to come. Taking our dinghy we left it hauled up, and all three walked over to the stranded yacht which was now lying at a steep angle on her bilge. The little family were clearly grateful to have us around while they dried themselves out and the wife brewed tea on a propped-up primus and gave the children, a fresh-faced little boy of seven and his sister a year or so younger, their first meal for a few hours.

While we talked, the youngsters with the resilience of kids were soon chasing each other happily about the hard sand. Ernest, a pleasant young fellow in his late twenties, told us how he had managed to get into this situation. He'd had only limited previous experience with small boats on the Medway before he'd bought this 24ft lifeboat hull, and had spent the last two years converting her into a neat looking cruising yacht, bolting an iron keel on to her which had come from an old yacht being broken up.

This was, he said, the first time that he and his family had ventured out of the Medway, where they kept her, and as it was their summer holiday and the weather had been so fine these past few days, with light south-easterlies, they had decided this was the time to sail across the Estuary to Harwich. His wife had relatives living at Dovercourt, he explained, and they were anxious for the children to see them and to show them their boat.

They had made the passage from Queenborough across the Thames as far as the East Swin pleasantly enough, with the wife and kids relatively happy and excited at being at last 'at sea'; but then the wind began to freshen and back more into the east, and suddenly fog came driving in from the sea. Almost immediately the distant shoreline was blotted out and the channel buoys disappeared. There was also the pronounced swell that we had encountered, and ere long the children were seasick and their mother, with hardly any experience of cruising and herself feeling little better, stayed in the cabin trying to comfort them.

The classic boating situation was rapidly developing where the family skipper is left to work the yacht alone in worsening conditions, while his family are laid low in the cabin and unable to be of any help to him. Ernest said he realised by now they had come too far to think of turning back, even though it would give them a fair wind back to the Medway, but he was uncertain of the various changes of course he would have to make in this poor visibility so as to keep away from the sands.

As he wrestled with the tiller he felt his little vessel was crying out to have a reef tucked in her mains'l and the stays'l taken off her, but he had never reefed before without someone at the helm, and he feared he might even fall overboard if he tried now. With the crumpled chart spread over his knees he attempted desperately to discover exactly where they were now, for all marks had long disappeared, and he knew he simply must find the Whitaker beacon or the Swin Spitway buoy so that he could find the channel leading between the sands into the more sheltered waters of the Wallet.

But strain his eyes as he might through the mist no lofty beacon or reeling buoy showed up, and after lurching and bashing along with the lee rail awash the little lifeboat found herself in the midst of a mass of breaking seas. Ernest thrust the helm down to stand off from what was evidently shallow water, but it was too late, and next moment came a series of sickening thuds and rattling shrouds that told him they were already on the sands. And the sudden heartburn the unhappy man felt was only made more intense by the cries of dismay from the cabin.

While he feverishly attempted to start the engine with the handle a sea broke against the yacht's quarter and gushed over into the cockpit, flooding the sparkplugs, and from that moment the engine was dead. In despair he clawed down the flogging sails while his boat bumped and lurched from side to side, and the waves continued to crash against her weather bilge.

At his wife's entreaties to call for help he started blowing the foghorn, but with little belief that the thin sound would be heard above the wind and the wash of the seas. Intense was their relief therefore when from somewhere out there to leeward they all heard a faint answering call. And then they could dimly make out the welcome shape of *Nightfall* and her russet sails as we brought up on the edge of the sand.

It seemed a long wait for all of us before the tide made sufficiently for their boat to lift, bumping heavily on her bilge, and finally float clear of the granite hard bottom. During all this time the weather was steadily worsening, and Bill and I aboard *Nightfall* were anxious lest the wind should back more into the north-east and give both yachts a dead beat against the flood tide past the Naze into Harwich. At any rate we were glad that Cliff had nobly volunteered to stay aboard the lifeboat to help out while we piloted them into the Orwell, and it was one other compensation that the sea fog was gradually clearing.

With a reef in the lifeboat's loose-footed mains'l, his small jib set and the little pram dinghy towing astern on a short painter,

Cliff and the family followed in our wake, well reefed down ourselves so as not to outrun them too far. Thus like weary homecomers our two yachts tossed and curtsied their way past the tower on the Naze cliffs, and stood into the bustle of Harwich Harbour as darkness began to settle over the restless sea. And in due time we led them up to Pin Mill where we were able to find them a vacant mooring near our own.

On the Monday morning the wind had backed as expected, and was blowing hard – more than half a gale – from the north-east. As our train hurried us back to London all three felt relieved to know that the family and their little ship were safe in the river now, and able to have the leak seen to on the hard.

"They were lucky their boat wasn't bilged and sunk before they floated off," mused Bill in his corner seat, "and only sprang a bad leak. Their little pram wouldn't have been much use to them in that sea."

"Must be a moral somewhere," said Cliff. "Ernest told me they'd hardly ever been outside the Medway or the Swale before, and I noticed his compass had a lot of deviation and hadn't been corrected. And I also had an awful job unchoking the bilge pump before we got to Harwich. There was no filter box and the pipe got choked with sawdust and muck. They really would have been in trouble if they'd been left on their own."

"Makes you think," said Bill before he dozed off, "how easy it can be for any inexperienced chap setting out to cross the Estuary to get himself into real difficulties, if he hasn't worked out all changes of courses through the channels beforehand, and noted them down for reference. You never know when the weather might cut up rough, or come in thick, do you?"

['. . . curtsied their way past the tower
on Naze cliffs'.]

– 7 –
A taste of the Western Isles

As evening approached and the fading light began to blacken the line of the great hills over the mainland, our game little yawl worked her way into an anchorage known only to my friends. While Stewart, a glistening figure in oilskins on the foredeck, conned his little ship, Rob steered her in towards the darkening shore while I took steady soundings with the leadline, feeling the weight of the lead bite into numb fingers as it still found no bottom. But suddenly the lead struck the ground.

"Nine fathoms, skipper."

"Aye, this'll do. Will ye get the main down now?"

The anchor was let go with a heavy splash and the cable allowed to rattle over the gypsy for some moments before Stewart dropped the pawl, while Rob and I clawed down the gaff and put a reasonably neat stow in the sodden folds of the mainsail. Our yawl brought up with a sudden snub, jerking the anchor chain for a moment out of the water in a straight line, then settling herself down as though surprised to find herself at anchor.

"Always like to feel the killick get a grand dig into the ground," said our Skipper. "I'll sleep the sounder the nicht."

The rain, intermittent all day, now drove past in earnest, and, with all made snug on deck, riding light hoisted on forestay and tiller pegged with a sheer away from the shore, we were all three glad to escape below, slam the hatch after us, and drop our dripping oilies in the fo'cs'le. And after Stewart had handed us both a man-size dram of Scotch and Rob had stoked up the cheerful little fire, the general air of icy dampness seemed to evaporate.

Stewart's shapely old gaff yawl, *Mora*, had all the traditional panelled mahogany opulence of the late Victorian era, within a deck length of some eleven metres, long overhangs, and a draught which would have had me generally on tenterhooks in the Thames Estuary. It had been at the invitation of my friends, both of whom worked in Glasgow, that I had travelled up from London eager to join them for a short cruise so that, as they said, they could show the East Coast sand dodger what sailing in the deep waters of their West Coast was really like.

In leisurely stages, therefore, from the moorings at Helensburgh we had sailed down the Clyde, rounded Toward Point in late afternoon, and let go our hook close to the Rothesay shore in the Kyles of Bute for the first night, while the crew fully enjoyed the beauty of the surrounding hills and the varying colours of the weed-covered rocks reaching down into the clear depths. With a moderate easterly breeze under a clear sky *Mora* rippled past Tighnabruaich and Ardlamont Point the next morning and headed south into Kilbrennan Sound, until we had brought the Cock of Arran and Lochranza abeam to port, and the peaks on the island, Beinn Breac and Beinn Tarsuinn, and their lesser fellows rose in ranks above the eastern skyline like dark bastions.

This spell of unexpectedly fine weather tempted us to carry on through the Sound along the rocky shore of the Kintyre Peninsular and round the Mull, but my two shipmates knew only too well how unpleasant it can be for small vessels the other side of the headland, should the weather change with its accustomed suddenness. *Mora* was accordingly put about and headed back towards Loch Fyne and the entrance to that hundred-mile shorter cut through the isthmus, the Crinan Canal.

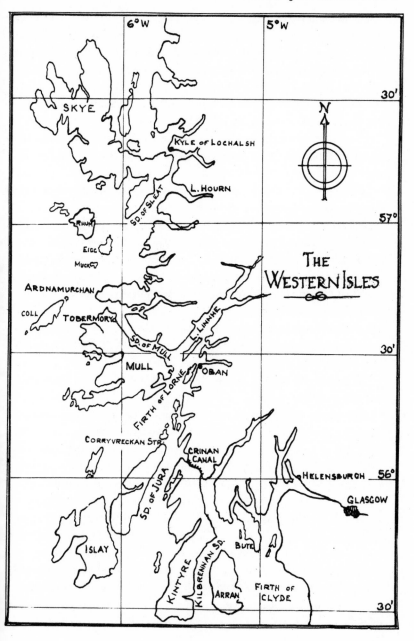

As she fetched along the Cowal shore with the wind a point free off the starboard bow, the breeze came crisp and scent-laden with heather and moss from a hundred miles or more across the Highlands. It recalled for me the familiar smell of marram grass and, in May perhaps, the fragrance of a field of beans beyond the wall of an Essex river: both scents heady and exciting, yet both so very different.

It was almost dark, and the breeze was slowly dying when we reached Lochgilphead and our yawl folded her wings for the night, ready to enter the canal in the morning.

When the lockgates opened with the dawn of another fine day, a Clyde puffer was the first to enter, followed closely by a large and very smart white ketch: an entirely appropriate sign of business before pleasure. It was only later as we tailed along astern of the white yacht that I understood Stewart's reluctance to press on too close to our leaders. To the accompaniment of the muffled clanging of a shovel below decks, the tall funnel of the puffer belched clouds of black smoke into the still air, and our amusement at the antics of the yacht's paid hand to keep his spotless decks and sail coats clear of the rain of smuts had to be disguised behind poker faces.

"Maybe yon owner comes from the South," was Stewart's only comment.

The Clyde puffer, with the exception I believe of one owned by a preservation society, is now an extinct species. With its high bluff bows and stumpy derrick mast forward, and its vertical boiler and tandem (monkey) compound engine tucked into the stubby round stern, the puffer used to be as familiar a sight in these waters as the spritsail barges in the Thames Estuary. And just as the barges were ousted by improved road services and modern motor coasters, so was the Clyde puffer.

An unhurried passage through this nine-mile cut is an enchanting experience on a fine day, for the canal passes through a pastoral landscape of lush green fields and dark woods of the Argyll isthmus, and except for the steady beat of *Mora*'s old Kelvin petrol-paraffin engine beneath our feet, there were few other sounds to break the still air. This canal, I had read in a book Rob handed me, was completed with its fifteen locks in 1801, largely as a result of the opening up of the Western Isles to trade, following General George Wade's great military road building achievements in the Highlands half a century before. It must have seemed a godsend to the skippers of the little sailing coasters of the time, avoiding the long haul round the Mull with its evil reputation.

At Crinan the puffer with its pall of smoke steamed out into a sea of glass, followed at a very discreet distance by the white ketch, while the smooth outline of Jura, Scarba and the nearer point of Craignish seemed to hang above their own reflections. There was no reason, we decided, to use up our fuel to reach any of the anchorages in the Firth of Lorne, but agreed that as Crinan Basin was a quiet place with only three other yachts in it, and a walk would do us all good, we stayed, and enjoyed instead a civilised and satisfying dinner at the Crinan Hotel.

. Browsing in my berth over the Clyde Cruising Club's excellent *Sailing Directions*, with its sketch charts of hundreds of little anchorages all over the West Coast, I came to realise what an astounding cruising ground the Scots can enjoy within reach of the Clyde. If all these islands and sheltered anchorages perchance lay within sixty miles of London, instead of Glasgow, I could not help thinking, what a playground the masses would have made of it: and yet, on our cruise so far we had encountered only half a dozen yachts under way.

With that suddenness for which the West Coast is noted, the weather changed overnight. The friendly area of high pressure over the Orkneys which had been bathing all Scotland in sunshine and easterly breezes these past few days, had moved on with the barometer dropping sharply. In the morning low clouds were coming before a freshening westerly wind from the Atlantic, and the islands we had seen the evening before were now obscured by a driving, icy rain – a wee mist, as Rob called it. I could tell we were in Scottish waters, for the damp air had a bit to it, a bone-freezing chill that found chinks in one's

clothing and carried a hint of Atlantic snows with it.

But our cruise must go on, and with her mainsail reefed, stays'l, and second jib set on the bowsprit and mizzen stowed, *Mora* stood out from Crinan Loch and, once clear of Ardnoe Point, began to thresh into the waters of Jura Sound, passing between the islands and, somewhere away to windward invisible in the rain, the mouth of Corryvreckan, that dreaded strait of whirlpools and turbulent waters on any weather-going tide. Thus after a damp and boisterous day's sailing our little yawl was conned round Duart Point on the tip of Mull, with the ancestral castle of the Maclean of Macleans guarding its bleak position, and sounded her way into Duart Bay for the night.

Next morning, with the wind still in the west, but not quite so strong and for the time being without rain, we fetched along the weather shore with the great expanse of the Sound of Mull opening out before us. A south-bound puffer passed us as we

['The great stretch of the Sound of Mull
opening before us']

brought Fishnish Point abeam to port, and Rob pointed out the
almost invisible entrance to Loch Aline on the Morvern shore
two miles away to leeward.

"That's a bonnie wee place for shelter from all winds," he
said, "except maybe sou'easterly. But we'll not put in there the
day."

Three years later I was to come this way again on my second
visit to the Scottish West Coast, with the owner of a 10.7 metre
ketch I had designed for him, and on that occasion we took her
into Loch Aline and found for ourselves what a snug and
beautiful anchorage it was for the peace-seeking small yacht.

Our intention today was to press on and, provided the
weather did not worsen or come in thick – as it so often can in
these parts – to get round Ardnamurchan Point and close in
with one or other of the small anchorages that Stewart knew in
Loch Moidart. But fate was to upset our plans in the shape of a

– 99 –

small motor boat with three line fishermen aboard, whose engine had broken down off Calve Island and who were drifing out into the broken waters of the Sound and towards the Morvern shore. To their wild signals and cries for help there was only one answer at sea: to stand by and render assistance, and tow them into Tobermory.

While Stewart and Rob talked to the three bedraggled beings in a language which seemed foreign to me, our faithful Kelvin gradually hauled their boat into the lee of the shore and through the narrows inside Calve Island to the anchorage below the town, while we inwardly cursed fools who went fishing on a breezy day without oars in their boat, or even a long enough anchor line.

It was too late now to think of pressing on round Ardnamurchan, and it was evident that we should have to settle for the night at Tobermory, and try our luck in the morning. The rain had set in again ("och, a wee mist"), it was Saturday night, and none of us had any hankering after a hotel bar in this little town of tourist attractions grouped in terraces round the harbour. As Stewart said, it wasn't worth taking the gripes off the dinghy, and we made ourselves comfortable with a dram or two, the fire burning cheerfully, and a good hot meal to follow.

To give a day to day, a blow by blow, account of any short cruise in home waters may make it sound very tiresome. Let it suffice that we were underway early with the wind still fresh from a little south of west, calling for one reef in the main, but with no more rain – for the time being. The Sabbath in these conditions seemed as good a day as any to get round the rocky headland of Ardnamurchan, where in the savage conditions of westerly gales so many ships have been wrecked in the past. With the white line of breakers fringing the rocky shore it looked a fearsome enough bastion to me, and as the white tower of the lighthouse came abeam I could not help thinking of the men who had built these stone towers which are scattered all around our coasts. I am afraid we sailing people tend to take all these lights for granted, like the buoys and beacons and the

['Into Tobermory Bay for a night of
rain']

good harbours that we can run into if we need. Yet in these
Northern waters all the seamarks, on wind-torn headlands and
wave-washed rocks, have been patiently erected, block by stone
block, by teams of men working in dangerous conditions as tide
and weather allowed them.

From early cressets of coal fires to candles in lanterns; then
smoky sperm oil wicks to the far brighter Argand circular
burner, until electricity brought today's brilliant light power,
the struggle for visible, reliable lights for the mariner has gone
on over the past three centuries. For those who would learn
more of how lighthouses were erected around these northern
outposts, like Pladda, Muckle Flugga, Mull of Galloway, Cape
Wrath or the Bell Rock for instance, *A Star for Seamen* by Craig

– 101 –

Mair tells the story of the remarkable Stevenson family of Edinburgh, generations of whom were engaged in building the scores of lighthouses round the coasts of Scotland, which are managed now by the Northern Lights Committee, the equivalent of the English Trinity House. When in his little yacht the anxious sailor first sights the distant light, he might recall what this books tells him, and offer up a prayer of thanksgiving for the men who worked and died so as to build and maintain such lights all over the world.

The wind held, and with freed sheets *Mora* dropped the miles astern as the rounded shapes of Muck and Eigg passed slowly to windward with the hills of Rum swelling the horizon beyond. Through the lee shrouds the smoke from Mallaig with its fish quays and canneries drifted away over the North Morar hills while the Point of Sleat came abeam to windward as we entered the Sound. We resisted the temptation to call it a day and tuck ourselves round the corner in Loch Nevis, but Stewart decided that Loch Hourn, a few miles farther on, would make a grand anchorage for the night.

He could not have chosen a more dramatic setting for his East Coast crew. When we turned into the Loch the lowering clouds hid the tops of the mountains on each side, seeming to shut us as in a great gloomy cavern, and as we rounded the first bend and got under the lee of the land even the water appeared to turn black. Loch Hourn, the loch of Hell, was silent and menancing, but it gave us a quiet if eerie night's anchorage. I shall always remember Loch Hourn.

Next day in pale sunshine we beat across the eight miles or so to Oronsay to replenish some stores, and then took the flood through puzzling swillies in Kyle Rhea, where the passage is less than a quarter of a mile wide between the Skye shore and the mainland. Our time was running out and this had to be our last anchorage before turning back for home. On a walk up to the high ground behind Kyleakin we stood with glasses, scanning the horizon towards the north-west down the Inner Sound, and could make out the outlines of Pabay, Longay,

Scalpay and the Crowlin islands, and beyond them the more distant hills of Raasay. Below the horizon would lie the bird-occupied Shiants and the Outer Hebrides: a fascinating cruising ground of scores of islands and numberless sheltered coves which called to us like syren voices. But our jobs to the south called a little harder.

The return from the apex of any cruise has a sense of sadness about it, and is usually someting of an anti-climax. Another depression came crowding in from the Atlantic and gave us a wet sail with a reef in the main and a choppy sea in the Sound of Sleat. A thin driving rain which seemed to me to penetrate with icy fingers everything we wore brought visibility down to half a mile as we came hard on the wind to clear Ardnamurchan, anxious not to get in too close.

The grisly headland loomed mistily through the rain, and the line of white breakers along the rocky shore alone put a chill in the heart: a cruel place for a small vessel to be dismasted. We were indeed relieved when we came under the lee of Ardmore Point on Mull, and put into Tobermory again for the night.

Next morning, with a rising glass and the wind more in the north west, still as cold as ever despite the pale sunshine, we enjoyed a last spanking sail to Oban, to leave *Mora* in charge of a boatman for Stewart to come and collect later with the rest of his summer holiday: aye, we agreed, it had been a bonnie wee cruise, and we hoped to manage another together, maybe some day.

More than fifty years have gone by since that last sail in the old *Mora*. There have been countless changes in the scene since then: the smoky puffers together with doubtless some of the few yachts we sighted will have disappeared, and you will probably find more than three yachts moored in Crinan Basin now. Yet the colours along the shore, the heather on the hills, and the sombre looming mountains must be as breathtaking as ever. And I dare say, when the wind comes northerly it still feels as though it is straight from the Arctic.

– 8 –

In search of colour

As we loosed the mainsail tiers the wind caught our oilskins and pressed them against the sail. The rain had stopped for a moment and the wavelets lifted their caps again, slapping the boat's topsides like mischievous children as she swung to the last of the flood. The *clink-clink* of the windlass quickened its tempo and the links of the chain dripped more hurriedly over the sheave.

"Anchor's atrip, Fid. Will you break out the jib?"

As I mopped down the foredeck my companion eased off the tripping line, and *Lone Gull* swung stern on to the wind, forging ahead towards the open sea. Over the sedge on Cobmarsh island he turned for a last glance at *Ben Gunn*, his own little 3-ton gaff sloop, whose mast stood saucily amongst the oyster smacks farther up Besom creek. But he was not saying goodbye to her for long.

"We'll soon have a find ebb under us, Maurice," he remarked as he crouched against the tiller lighting his pipe between cupped hands. "A fair wind and a fair tide. Couldn't want anything better, could we?"

He was right. Cold, wet and windy though it was for this time of year, yet it was in our favour as we ran down Mersea Quarters bound for – we knew not where. That is what made Fid Harnack such a good shipmate. He never complained at what kind of a cruise we embarked on: he would be as ready for a cruise to the Channel Islands or the Frisian group as for the few days of restful pottering we had promised ourselves during this last week in August. I had just finished writing a longish book with a historical setting which had meant a good deal of research work, and was feeling mentally exhausted, while he had brought his water-colour materials along and looked forward to a gentle loaf from day to day as we felt inclined, looking for pictures worth sketching and leaving each day's plans to the morning itself.

Rounding up below the last of the anchored yachts, we set the mainsail. How good it felt to grasp the halyard and run the tanned sail up as though it had been a large blind, to be able to swig it taut with just a few turns of the mast winch: how satisfying to stand coiling the staysail halyards and to look up at the rich full curves of the sail against the sky, to hear the bow wave beneath one's feet rise to a cheerful roar as the little ship thrust her way through the water.

Lone Gull seemed to respond to my expectant mood. It was, after all, her first season and she was still new and a little frolicsome. Her plans had been conceived the previous September aboard the Cunarder when I was on my way to America to cover Tom Sopwith's challenge with his second *Endeavour* for the America's Cup. While I sketched out in in my cabin the preliminary lines I could not help laughing at the world of difference between my beamy, shallow-draught centreboard conception and the two great J-Class greyhounds that were to meet off Rhode Island, the Charles Nicholson-designed *Endeavour* II and the Starling Burgess and Olin Stevens-created *Ranger*. The defender once more was to prove decidedly the faster of the two, and while I brought back my plans, duly influenced by various American designers whom I was enabled to meet, the Cup remained in its New York Yacht Club home until, as it turned out, an Australian challenger was to win it and take the 133-year-old trophy away 47 years later.

Apart from her rig with its bermudian mainsail, boomed

working staysail and Wykeham Martin furling jib set on only a short bowsprit, there was more than a hint of the local cockle bawleys in *Lone Gull*'s wide shallow hull and deep bulwarks when she eventually took shape in Johnson and Jago's yard at Leigh-on-Sea. Measuring 28.4ft on deck, 25.0ft on the water-line with 10.0ft beam and 3.3ft draught with the wooden built-up centreboard raised, she was a handy, comfortable packet for the shallow waters of the Thames Estuary.

"The Blackwater looks pretty grey today," I remarked, coming aft with the sail tiers. "Like slate."

My marine artist friend turned to look back at our wake.

"If you mixed paint to get that shade," Fid told me thoughtfully, "you'd have to use a lot of blue."

"A lot of blue paint to get *that*?"

He nodded, smiling through his spectacles. And I looked more carefully at the hurrying water. Until then it had seemed to me to be one with the sky: drab, dull, unrelieved grey. Yet as I followed Fid's directions and looked with greater understanding I could see that he was right. There was indeed more than a hint of blue in all that grey sky and water. Queer that I hadn't noticed that the first time.

Colne Bar buoy with its ball-like topmark was slowly weaving in the tide as we left it to starboard and, for the sake of form more than caution, leaded our way across the shingle banks close in to Colne Point. Somehow the presence of a centreboard ballasted a little with an iron shoe gave one confidence that at about a fathom we had an instant sounding device.

The ebb was running fairly hard now and the beach by Jaywick was slipping past at a great rate. But the wind was veering and already we had the sheets almost close-hauled. The afternoon was not getting any brighter, and the squalls were if anything colder than they had been during the morning.

With the low sandstone cliffs of Holland Gap nearly abeam, the breeze suddenly flew into the north and came at us with an unexpected viciousness. Soon *Lone Gull* was carrying too much canvas with her whole mainsail set. Her scuppers were beginning to gurgle, and any more weight in the wind would have her lee decks wet, and for a wide-beamed boat like *Lone Gull* that would imply that things were not altogether how they ought to be.

"Ease her up a bit, Fid, while I tuck a few rolls in the main."

Even as I sat astride the mast turning the reefing handle with the main halyard eased round the winch barrel, the squalls gathered in weight, and I continued turning like an old-fashioned organ grinder until there were three good rolls in the main. Then we furled the jib with its tricing line and let the ship carry on under reefed mainsail and staysail. A stinging cold rain came driving out of the north, blotting out the end of the Naze and leaving the Gunfleet pile light on the other side of the sands a small blur away to the east.

"Not fit for humans on deck now," I said, looking around for any signs of other craft, but there was none in sight. "It'll be warmer below – and, anyway, everything stops for tea."

With the tiller pegged to keep her on course, we left the ship to look after herself, and went below. Peeling off our oilskins in the cosy cabin, we were grateful for the warmth. With the cabin doors closed it seemed as though we were far removed from the rush of wind and sea and general racket outside, although through the large oval port in the galley I could see the steep little crests tumbling past, and every now and then catch a glimpse of *Hickey*, the dinghy, above the after coaming lifted over one and snatched forward by the taut painter.

It was some years since I had been inveigled to sea in a deep, narrow-gutted yacht, and it was difficult to remember clearly the fatigue and discomfort that go with a boat that too often sails with her covering board awash. With her beam and wide cabin sole one could walk about *Lone Gull*'s cabin even when she was sailing hard, and today it was a joy to be able to leave her to it, threshing away close-hauled with the tiller held fast, and to prop oneself against the after part of the centreboard case – which separated the companion steps from the galley – while making the tea.

Off the Naze, amongst the confused seas over the Stone Banks, it was a dead nose-ender up towards Harwich, and there was still a fierce ebb pouring out of the Harbour against us. It would be plain pigheadedness, we both agreed, to go on beating up into the Harbour, making very little each board against the tide, when a far more restful and attractive anchorage lay a few miles to the south-westward of us.

With sheets eased, therefore, and the cold wind now on her starboard quarter, *Lone Gull* stormed past the Pye End buoy up to the windswept solitude of Hamford Water. And when we let go the anchor close up to the edge of Pewit Island a flight of duck was the only sign of life near us. The world seemed to be ours.

Before the light began to fade Fid took his sketch-pad out into the cockpit, and sat making two or three little pencil studies of the nearby sedge bank on the island with the high ground and trees beyond, and a neat little note of the Island Point buoy with its odd topmark at the entrance to Walton Channel. Then it became too cold for further outside work, or else the smell of supper warming on the top of the bogie stove had its magnetic effect.

Like an unwanted guest, the chill north wind was still with us next morning, but the sun had broken through and the sky was a deep blue with clouds racing across it like puffs of yellow smoke. The world had arrayed itself in bright colours once more, and the crisp air made one feel good to be alive and afloat. The young flood was beginning to cover the Pye Flats when we got underway and edged our course past the reeling High Hill buoy. A distinct swell was coming in from the sea, suggesting that there was plenty of wind somewhere to the north, and running up across the sands against the wind.

"Do you see how the crests are breaking to *windward*" said Fid, pointing, "and the spume is being blown back over them? That would make a good picture in oils."

While he dug out his sketching block again I kept the ship as close up to the weather side of the channel as I dared, and watched him make a hurried sketch of the scene: the bluff mass of the Naze in the distance, the glint of the sun through the clouds, the black buoys marking the edge of the channel, and the swell tumbling in across the sands at an angle to the wind waves, with their crests curled over and blown back against the run of the sea. It was a charming sketch even in the rough, and the finished oil painting which I saw later on was, I thought, one of Fid's best.

"Do you see what colour your forehatch is, Maurice? Look at that, now."

Fid laid his sketch block down and pointed. The forehatch, hinged aft on the cabin top which was extended forward of the mast, was propped up at an angle of perhaps twenty degrees to catch the air below. From where we sat in the cockpit the blue of the sky was reflected on the glossy surface of the varnish. The rich red of the mahogany underneath had been transformed by the blend of colours.

"Why, it looks quite – er – mauve to me."

"Yet if you painted it that colour," said my artist friend wistfully, "most people would say you were exaggerating your tones. But I'll make a note of it, all the same, and show you."

For the next quarter of an hour I watched him work with his water colours in swift, deft strokes of the brush, bringing out the essence of the tints reflected on the hatch. I was so absorbed in the work that I nearly ran into the big Cliff Foot cage buoy at the entrance to the Harbour, and decided to pay more attention to where I was steering. But during the long beat up the Orwell with the wind becoming more and more north-westerly and flukey, I watched my friend making quick colour roughs of the ever-changing views, mixing seemingly impossible colours on his palette and yet blending them to just the shades of te trees and grassland ashore, the colours in the smoke from the steamer at the buoys in Butterman's Bay, and the rich tan of the barges' sails lightering cargo alongside her. Watching his deft strokes forming the steamer's rusty hull and bridge structure, I recalled that he had worked frequently with that master

['Past the big steamer discharging at
the buoys']

marine artist, the late Arthur Briscoe, whose house in Coast
Road overlooked the Mersea anchorage. It was, I believe, at
Briscoe's urging that at one time, when he was still a young
budding painter, Fid had made a voyage in the barque *Alastor*
and learnt something of a ship at sea and her rigging and gear,
and perhaps learnt something, too, of the older artist's style.

With the last of the flood we crept past the dark red Tudor
tower at Freston and up to the New Cut above Bourne creek,
and opened up the view of the lock gates leading into the docks
at Ipswich. Cutting off a wide sweep westward in the old
channel, where some of the local boats lay at half-tide moorings, this cut was dug in 1842 when the new wet dock was
completed, the largest of its kind in the country at the time, and
Ipswich made itself an important seaport for ships up to 3000
tons or so. Any vessel too large to go through the lock had to

bring up on the moorings in the reach below Pin Mill – how it got the name Butterman's Bay, I know not – and discharge her cargo into barges or lighters. Since then new quays have been built and extended on both sides of the river leading up to the lock, and much larger container ships and vehicle carriers, wearing all the hideous angularities of the modern age, sweep up and down the narrow channel to Continental ports.

As we slowly approached in the dying breeze a deep-laden steamer was being warped out from the newly constructed quay, and while I jilled the ship around Fid transferred her massive bulk to paper, taking her from various angles as she insinuated herself into the channel, and reproducing exactly the dark red stains of rust that streaked her iron sides. And when she had passed down the river beneath a rising cloud of smoke, and two barges followed slowly in her wake, their tan sails reflected peacefully in the water, we picked a berth amongst the fleet of little vessels at the mouth of Ostrich creek. The ebb began to flow silently towards the sea, and as we sat in the cockpit having tea it felt good to let the world drift by like the tide, unchecked, almost unnoticed. With the passing of the hour of high water the life of the river seemed to subside and the long reach down past Freston and Woolverstone was deserted, save for the buoys whose twinkling lights would soon pierce the growing shadows.

In the still of the evening we climbed into the dinghy, and, as I rowed slowly up the little creek while the drops of water fell off the oar blades in tiny whispers, Fid sat in the sternsheets busy with the sketch-pad on his knee. He made a note of the arched brick road bridge across the creek before we passed beneath it, and another quick sketch of the ancient Ostrich inn on the other side of the road. The roar of a train grew in volume as it ran down the incline from Belstead and clattered past us along the embankment, dying away as it rounded the curve towards Stoke tunnel. I could not suppress a chuckle when I recalled that once, during my early days in Ipswich, a young school pal who shared my love of trains joined me in trespas-

sing on the London line to see just how the engines of the fast
Norwich trains picked up water in their tenders while rushing
past at 50 or 60 miles an hour. Undetected we found the
quarter-mile-long troughs with water in them between the rails
not far from this spot, and just had to sit beside the line and
wait for the non-stop Norfolk Coast Express to come roaring
down from London. As the train came over the troughs we had
a front row view of the scoop lowered beneath the tender, but
had not reckoned on the shower of spray that drenched us both
as the wheels thundered by, while we rolled about shouting
with laughter. But it mattered not to us, for it was true *railway*
water and so almost sacred to us; but it took us both a long time
to dry off enough to face our respective mums!

The early morning was still and misty. The reflections of the
trees on either shore lay motionless, and those same channel
buoys seemed to stand like sentinels above the water, lifted
above their own reflections by the haze. Another ebb had
flowed past us during the night, and there was not enough of it
left for us to set our sails and drift, as we should have liked,
placidly down and waiting for the breeze that the day promised. It is some ten miles down to the harbour mouth, and we
felt we should like to take the next flood somewhere towards the
Crouch. With the Gray engine purring at half-throttle, therefore, we ran down past the Pin Mill anchorage, where many of
the yachts still had their riding lights burning, and on past the
same steamer lying at the buoys in the Bay.

At Colimer Point the ebb was nearly done. The great cage
buoy lay motionless as though set in glass, and even the fuss
that our dinghy was making at the end of its painter passed the
iron sides in a series of slaps without waking the monster. Then
on down Sea Reach and a first glimpse of the skyline of Harwich and the sea beyond: how vivid is my memory of the very
first time I saw that, when as a callow youth with no experience
of sailing I had managed to sail my own little yacht and, by
devious and hair-raising manoeuvres, navigate her safely down
from the ancient port to this sight of – the Sea!

How well I knew every mud bank and buoy and bight in the Orwell where my first years of sailing had been spent. And even now, leaving a harbour as the sun is setting, bound on a passage, however modest (and most of my night passages have been modest enough), never fails to recapture those early joys of sensing adventure. That is one of the everlasting pleasures of sailing small craft: the actual feel of the halyards, the sound of the anchor windlass, the creak of the blocks, the ripple of the water at the stem, the life that springs in the tiller as the little ship turns and heads seaward – none of these things has ever lost its magic as the years have gone by. As flying into the dawn in a jet plane is to the experienced air pilot, so getting underway in a small ship is to the cruising yachtsman, however many times each has done it before.

We caught the flood tide. It is true that the engine alone made it possible, for the last three miles past Shotley and the mouth of the Stour, past the old seaplane base at Felixstowe and then the very end of the land at Landguard, were a steady push against the incoming flood. But once outside the harbour the tide was beginning to curve out towards the Naze and carrying us with it, while a light northerly air was keeping the mainsail quiet and filling the folds of our white ghoster jib. With two laden barges bound south in company with us, we appeared to have the sea to ourselves, for the Flushing packet which was rapidly overhauling the three of us from her berth at Parkeston would soon round the Beach End bell buoy and sheer away to port on her course for Holland. Quiet though our engine was, it was with the usual relief that we were able to stop it, and let *Lone Gull* forge her almost silent way over the gentle swell with her sails drawing nicely.

In the light breeze we steadily overhauled the two barges, and as we almost imperceptibly drew ahead of the second of them – *Phoenician*, one of Cranfield's smartly-kept fleet from Ipswich – Fid busied himself making a dozen or more thumbnail sketches of her from all angles, while I steered first to one side of her then the other, studying the heart-warming curves in her hull and sails and rigging. It is the only way, as any marine artist will tell you, to draw convincing pictures of a Thames barge that will look right to a seaman. But oh, what travesties of spritsail barges can be seen in almost any local art exhibition on the East Coast!

The breeze held and slowly we made the Crouch before the first of the ebb began to hold us back. Choosing a place on the far side of the Burnham anchorage where there were no moorings, we let go our hook (with a stout line and buoy attached to its crown, just in case it did come foul) and rowed around the anchorage while Fid sketched the more graceful of the yachts – and how few are graceful at both ends! – before we went ashore to the quay for fresh bread.

In the evening on the last of the day's ebb we drifted down towards Shore Ends, drinking in the scents that were wafted off the meadows by the light breeze, and listening to the gentle sounds of farmlands – the lowing of cows in a field, a dog barking in the distance, the sudden *plop* of a fish jumping inshore of us, the cracked bell in the Burnham town clock striking the hour. The river became wrapped in darkness before we had leaded our way in towards the north bank just inside the mouth, to sleep the sleep of the tired amid the stillness under the glow of our riding light, until the next flood tide would be coming in and filling the channels.

The sun was barely above the horizon when we broke out the anchor as the little ship was beginning to turn to the first of the ebb. It was our last day, and we wanted to work our tides as though we had no mechanical help hidden beneath the steps into the cabin. Fid's 20ft *Ben Gunn*, which he and his brother had converted into a neat little cabin sloop back in 1921, had never been fitted with an auxiliary engine; while my own introduction to boat ownership that same year had been with an engineless cutter, and the next three boats owned in succession had all been without mechanical power, other than muscle and a long oar or sweep.

In our different ways, therefore, we both had learnt the hard way to sail boats and all that boatmanship implied, and even now preferred to use the sails rather than rely on an engine to move the yacht. For us older yachtsmen there is great satisfaction in working our boats around the coast, in and out of creeks and anchorages, using the tides to every advantage, instead of motoring everywhere with sails folded. For nearly five thousand years seamen had navigated their craft over the Mediterranean, the Red Sea, the Indian Ocean and the waters of Northern Europe, with nothing but their sails, aided on occasion by oars, and in time when the invention of the rudder hinged on the sternpost was followed by that of the navigator's compass, ships with nothing but sails to drive them explored the oceans of the world and formed the new trade routes. Steam, petrol or diesel or gas turbine engines have become a huge improvement in driving big ships around the Seven Seas, but small vessels can still usually get where they want using only the winds of Heaven.

For the sailing man, however, the advent of yacht marinas, where it is inadvisable – if not forbidden – for the danger of damage to other yachts, to enter or leave a berth under sail, except in ideal conditions, has resulted in a general lack of ability in many owners to use sails at all. Even the art, or technique, of dropping one's anchor properly so that it will not become foul, has never been fully learnt by many owners of today's shiny and highly expensive yachts. With a yacht marina in almost every river the need to use one's anchor at all has become a rarity.

The chill northerly wind had gone, and in its place the gentlest of breezes from the south-east ruffled the surface of the water. With her ghoster just lifting its sheet clear of the water, and her mainsail almost lifeless, *Lone Gull* moved through the water without a murmur, while we had our breakfast and talked of days we had both endured in the past, when these waters were lashed into a seething mass of white crests and our little ship had heeled and plunged, her lee rail buried and her bowsprit dripping water as it rose again towards the sky. With a harsh easterly these waters outside the mouth of the Crouch can be a welter of unpleasantness when you are forced to make a passage.

As we continued to drift with the ebb down the Rays'n taking care to keep well to the westward over the Dengie side of the channel so as not to be carried over onto the Buxey Sand as the ebb sets across it, the beacon slowly came into view through the morning mist. Its topmark, like four arms of a crossroads signpost, was a familiar sight to us then, but in recent years the beacon has been updated, like the Whittaker and others around the coast, in accordance with the international buoyage system, and it shows today two superimposed cones above a massive steel pile.

The sun grew stronger and the decks were warm to the feet. But the breeze sighed into oblivion, the little catspaws grew fitful and shy, and the water became a mirror on which the little ship floated without apparent motion. But over the sandy bottom a few feet beneath our centreboard we knew our shadow was silently drifting north-eastwards with the tide, slowly but inexorably, while the dinghy's painted drooped in the water.

Sensing a picture ('Yacht in a Calm' perhaps?) Fid took the dinghy and sculled himself astern a few yards with his watercolour box and painting pad. While the skipper sat pretending to steer, dressed in sunhat and shorts, Fid worked away in silent concentration. Soon he held out the result for me to see: a charming colour study of the scene, perfect in its reflections of *Lone Gull* on the water, with his own *Ben Gunn* becalmed about half a mile away. The final watercolour now hangs above the typewriter in my study, and is a faithful reminder of those few wonderful days we had together looking for colour on the East Coast.

By degrees the Buxey beacon came abeam, and as slowly passed under the starboard quarter. The water was shoaling and one could see the ripples on the sand beneath our keel. We should soon be feeling the ebb pouring out of the Blackwater and if no breeze came, I was thinking, the anchor would have to be let go to hold us from drifting down the coast past Clacton.

"There's a breeze coming," said Fid as he clambered aboard again, and within a few minutes it was upon us, rippling the surface, filling the ghoster and lifting the parts of the mainsheet well clear of the water, and sending me hurrying below to put on some more clothes. It was indeed chill, coming in from the sea, but entirely welcome, and it brought our little ship to her senses; and as it strengthened on our starboard quarter we headed towards the Blackwater for one last joyous sail before the rollicking wavelets.

The colours in the water changed, the dun shade over the flats took on a greenish hue that deepened in the clearer water of the river, and soon the green was speckled with white crests which flashed in the sun. Some of the oyster smacks were coming out from Mersea, and we watched them admiringly as with their mainsails partly triced up the mast, their brown staysails drawing strongly, and the usual small jib set halfway along the long bowsprit, they came towards us tack by tack on their way to the fishing grounds. A splendid sight for the man who likes workboats under sail.

Soon we were through them while they worked their way out to windward, the spray from their powerful bows flashing every now and then in the sun, while we rounded the Nass beacon back to our anchorage in the Quarters.

"I shall always remember these few days," I said while we sat in the cockpit looking round at the familiar scene, "for all the simple things we've seen and enjoyed. And I think I have learnt some things about colours in painting that I never guessed before. And yet for many people we have just idled, wasted five precious days ditch-crawling, when we might have sailed over to Holland and back."

"It has suited me," said Fid complacently. "It's given me an opportunity to fill in a lot of notes in my book, like those barges out of Harwich, for instance."

"Next year," I mused, "if I can manage ten days or a fortnight early in September, I think we might sail over and sketch Belgian and Dutch fishing boats and harbours on the other side. I've not taken *Lone Gull* foreign yet. What do you say?"

"That's a date, Skipper."

But when that next September came around and *Lone Gull* was getting prepared for her first cruise to the other side, events in Europe changed all our lives, leaving the little ship with a sad heart to be laid up in her builders' yard for the next six years.

And when we were demobilised and returned to our respective jobs, and *Lone Gull* was once more brought to life and got ready for the projected Dutch cruise, she had acquired a new mate, Coppie, who trustingly had everything to learn about little ships and sailing.

– 9 –
Over to Holland

'And if you cared to leave *Lone Gull* in the Sixhaven at Amsterdam,' the letter read, 'we shall be pleased if you join us for a week or so in the *Maartje* which we have chartered for a month. Hedda and I will most like to show you as many of the fishing ports of the Ijsselmeer as we can visit in the time. Do please come.'

Our Dutch friends' invitation was too good an opportunity to miss, offering us the experience of sailing a real fishing botter in its home waters. Vries, I knew, had sailed many times as a boy with the fishermen on the Zuider Zee, before the north polder had been built and enclosed it, and from the time I had first met him in 1944, when he was a lieutenant-commander in the Royal Netherlands Navy and I was an RNVR bloke, I had realised that sailing was as much in his blood as it was in mine.

Fid Harnack, my artist friend, was enthusiastic over the scheme, for it would be a chance to sketch and paint local craft in their Dutch harbours. Our plans for *Lone Gull*'s first cruise after the war were to explore the Dutch waterways, and Coppie, the new mate, looked forward to cruising in the Lowlands where, she thought, there must at least be smooth sailing. It was therefore a great idea to sail over to the Hook, make our way via Rotterdam, Gouda and the inland route to Amsterdam, leave our own ship in the yacht harbour there, the Sixhaven, and join Vries and Hedda for a week of our holiday.

With rationing of nearly all commodities still in force, even a fortnight's cruise like this had to be planned with care. We knew our friends in Holland were still suffering from shortages worse than ours, indeed from six gruesome years of German occupation, reprisals and wanton destruction, and we were determined to take them whatever stores we could gather together. Happily, when she was built before the war, I had had *Lone Gull* registered as a British Ship like any merchant vessel, and now discovered that this entitled us to draw seaman's rations for the ship's company of three for a voyage lasting up to three weeks.

Certain forms when completed in quadruplicate led us to a warehouse in London's dockland which wore the aroma of an old-time grocer's. Here was a veritable Aladdin's cave where we found we were able to draw from the stacked shelves foodstuffs that housewives had not seen for years: canned meats and grade one red salmon, peaches and pineapple in syrup, sealed tins of coffee, sticks of naval cocoa-in-milk, big bars of chocolate, cooking oil galore, ship's biscuits, lifeboat stores in sealed tins, spirits, beers and tobacco (Fid the only smoker aboard). Seamen's allowances seemed at that time overwhelmingly generous, but we knew our friends in Holland would be glad to share them.

Lone Gull's petrol engine had been somewhat temperamental of late, reluctant to start and inclinded to stop for no evident reason, as if it too had not quite recovered from the war years. While we lay at anchor off Harwich town quay for the Customs officer to come aboard to check our bonded stores, a local garage mechanic lay outstretched on the cabin sole working on the machinery, uttering unintelligible comments from time to time. At last he rose and, wiping his hands sweatily, declared "It's okay now, it's American, but I've fixed it," and let the engine roar its head off for a while just to prove it.

The forecast had been west-north-westerly winds, fresh to strong, but the wind could not have been more fair for our

['*Lone Gull* . . . leaving the Dovercourt
Lights astern']

course almost due east from the Cork light vessel to the Hook,
and with a dateline to meet at Amsterdam we were already
fretting like race-horses at the starting post to be off. It seemed
our going must be now or never.

It was evident that the passage was not going to be a smooth
one, and to avoid what might be a traumatic experience for
someone whose only previous connection with boats and the
sea had been her Boat Wrens at Portsmouth during the war, it
was arranged for Coppie to go over on the night ferry from
Parkeston Quay and to meet us, hopefully, at the Royal Maas
Yacht Club in Rotterdam.

As soon as the Customs man and the magician had boarded

their launch, taking a somewhat wistful-faced Coppie with them, our anchor was hove up, sail set – two rolls in the main, small jib and stays'l – and *Lone Gull* was bustling out of the Harbour and leaving Dovercourt Old Lights astern like a frightened hare. With her dinghy lashed bottom up inside the starboard rail we had no anxiety on that score – no surging up on the following seas, no worry about parting the painter and losing the little boat – and as the low cliffs of the Suffolk coast dropped astern and we streamed the log, we settled ourselves down to what promised to be a fast run down wind.

"That bank of cloud to wind'ard is worth noting," remarked Fid, opening his sketchbook. And while he busied himself in making a quick sketch, sitting with his back to the bulkhead, I kept a weather-eye lifting over my shoulder at the ominous mass of black rising above the western horizon like a range of mountains. Soon the wind was piping up in earnest and the tiller puller harder.

"Take her, Fid, will you, while I get a few more rolls down?"

Blessing the invention of the worm roller gear which enabled me to reef the mainsail while still running before the wind, I thought of the old Bristol Channel pilot cutters which had introduced it first as the Appledore gear, making it possible for one man on occasion to sail a heavy 25-tonne cutter home by himself when the other pilots had been put on board incoming ships. With the jib taken off her, and under the stays'l and main with six rolls in it, *Lone Gull* felt easy and snug and ready to take on anything the western sky felt like flinging at us in mid-July.

From unhappy experiences in the past, or possibly from the effects of six years at war, I had become much more cautious than formerly, and felt that with a sky like that to windward and evening closing in it was easier to adopt the old rule of the East India Company's ships and snug down at nightfall. It is only too easy when running downwind not to notice how much the wind is increasing, and to carry on for too long; for the yacht's speed takes that much off the apparent speed of the wind – and its weight – until it can become too late to round up into the wind so as to put in more reefs, or heave-to. Many fine ships in the days of sail have been overwhelmed, almost driven under, and lost through a captain's insistence on carrying on for too long.

Fid and I agreed on playing it safe for tonight, and as it turned out it was the right thing to do. Just before dark, when the double flash of the Sunk light vessel was almost caressing the horizon astern of us, and the young moon showed herself every now and then racing between the banks of cloud, the wind piped up more than ever. The seas, beginning to look black now, with every so often a gleaming crest blown forward in spray, were beginning to build up. Probably because the tide was running across the wind, instead of directly against it, the seas were not quite so steep as I have known them in the North Sea, and at least so far a fair distance from crest to crest.

Lone Gull raced before them like an old lady chased by a bull. With her generous beam and long straight keel, and her board hauled right up, she was a comfortable old thing in these conditions, running straight and true with little tendency to sheer to port or starboard. And her flat mid-sections, like those of the oyster smacks, effectively damped down any rolling before it could build up into that exhausting bugbear of so many tender deep-keeled yachts – the swinging, rhythmic roll.

We set our watches, and through the night took two-hourly spells. For a short day – night passage like this it has proved a good arrangement: the man off watch can produce hot drinks or sandwiches for both hands, while able to catch an hour or more's sleep, yet ready to turn out at a moment's call. To have something to eat at two-hourly intervals helps to keep any queasiness at bay, although *Lone Gull*'s motion didn't affect either of us in this way.

For the helmsman, sitting comfortably with legs out-stretched and an arm over the tiller from where he could see over the coachroof forward, steering for a couple of hours was no great chore. The compass, in full view through an open window in the cabin bulkhead, was lit from above by a small light bulb enclosed inside a metal cylinder. Through a thin slit in the bottom of the brass, which was adjustable, a ray of light about half an inch wide fell across the compass card lighting up the lubber's line, which was clear enough for the helmsman without any diffusion or dazzle.

"She's certainly tramping along," Fid remarked once as his dark form emerged into the cockpit to take over another two-hour trick. "What's the log say?"

"68 miles."

"Then she's done about 12½ miles in your watch, Maurice. That's better than 6 knots, and we're not pressing her."

It was indeed grand sailing through the night like this, able to make out the heaping seas astern as they advanced with their greenish white crests tumbling, and to feel the heave as one lifted our stern, carried us boiling along with it until the crest seemed to hover amidships, then feel the ship slowly sink again as the wave roared ahead of us, foam-flecked on each side of the bow in the red and green glow of our side lights. It was a wonderful night to be at sea with the wind fair, if boisterous withal, and I felt glad I had sent the mate over on the packet. Conditions such as this could easily have put her off cruising for ever: we have all known it happen to other couples.

Daylight brought a bright sky and a green, white-flecked tumbling sea, while the wind drew more to the westward and continued to blow as hard as ever. We could not help thinking what it would have been like trying to punch the other way all night long against these seas: the violent pitching, the cold driving spray, the deadly slow progress, the near impossibility to prepare a satisfying hot meal. Perhaps we both lack the sterner stuff that makes hard-core sailors and offshore racing yachtsmen. I for one take my hat off to them, but for my kind of boat-owner partnership, like *Lone Gull* I think fair winds are a heaven-sent gift, and worth waiting for!

The low coastline, punctuated with groups of buildings, a church spire, tall chimneys and here and there a water tower, came up over the horizon under the sun, and almost over the

['It was the buoy marking the
mine-swept ship channel']

bowsprit a great tall pillar buoy seemed suddenly to rise out of
the seas, reeling, twisting and falling with the water cascading
off its black sides. As it swept past we read its name, HK 13,
and rejoiced inordinately, for with our log now reading 106
miles from the Cork light vessel our little ship had unerringly
hit off our target, the buoy marking the mine-swept ship channel a few miles off the entrance to the Hook.

The *Sailing Directions*, we recalled, warned small craft not to
approach in any strong onshore winds until at least two hours'
flood had made, as 'on the ebb a dangerous sea can break over a
distance of a mile or more from the entrance', and Fid checked
the tide tables, sucking at his pipe.

"As I see it," he said at last, "low water at the Hook was half and hour ago. It'll be another half-hour at least before we get there, right? So the flood should have made about an hour, which shouldn't be too bad, should it?"

Wearing stiff upper lips in traditional British manner we stood on. The nearer we approached the land the whiter looked the line of breakers off the piers, and doubtless the whiter our own gills. This strong westerly wind was certainly teasing the sea, even though as Fid had calculated the young flood was already running in, and soon *Lone Gull* found herself in the midst of some steep breakers which were noisier and angrier as they raced up astern than any we had ridden during our 21-hour passage. The sensible advice in the *Directions*, to wait until at least two hours' flood, was borne in upon us, for it was evident that the great outflow of this vast river, the Lek, which stretched almost a hundred and fifty miles across Holland into Germany, continued to pour down into the sea against at least the first two hours of the flood tide. And while we danced and gyrated through what was very like a small race, we pondered what it could be like on the full ebb with a westerly gale blowing: no wonder, we reflected, small fishing craft and a yacht or two have been lost at the Hook.

With our decks drying off our progress up the first mile or two of this New Waterway was noticeably slowed by the outflowing current, then gradually this eased and we began to make good time before the wind which seemed now to be easing until we were able to unroll first two, and later all five rolls in the mainboom. Before this waterway was completed during the 1880s the approach to Rotterdam had been through the Oude Maas and past the old town of Brielle and the East Plaat, a winding and difficult channel even for the steamers of that day. Then with the opening of this straight cut a new port at its entrance – de Hoek van Holland – with rail links to the rest of the Continent offered the packet boats from Harwich and the Thames a shorter and quicker service. And, nestling close behind the quays at the Hook a little fishing port, Berghaven, was to prove a welcome shelter for us later during this cruise.

As the flat countryside – if that is now the description of this energetic industrialised land – slipped past and the towers and chimneys and giant dockyard cranes of Rotterdam hove into view, the traffic on the river grew more intense and crowded. Overtaken by freighters and motor barges, dodging ferries and outward-bound ships, *Lone Gull* found herself leaping over the wash-fretted waters of one of the busiest waterways in the world. With so much happening around us Fid worked with sketchbook in hand making dozens of rapid notes for use with future illustrations and paintings.

Towering over the quayside buildings on our starboard bow, the bold, flaring black hull of a great liner was slowly detaching itself from the quay under the straining hawsers of two smart diesel tugs, her glossy sides contrasting with her white upper-works and the two large buff funnels with broad green-white-green bands of the Holland-Amerika line. Fid told me about her.

"*Nieuw Amsterdam*", he said. "She was built at that shipyard over there just before the war. She's about 36,600 tons. A fine handsome ship, isn't she?" And all her vital statistics with his sketches of her were to be included in the next edition of that handy mine of inforation, *All About Ships and Shipping*, which his brother E P (Gus) Harnack, edited and Fid profusely illustrated over many years.

Amidst this turmoil of bustling vessels and choppy water sails seemed to be an anachronism, and in deference *Lone Gull* quietly lowered hers while, after several grinding-starter attempts, the engine sprang into life. But as she edged up to the entrance to the yacht harbour beside the Royal Maas Yacht Clubhouse it lost its nerve, faltered and cut out, and wouldn't start again.

Under the hurriedly set stays'l, with muttered imprecations against reluctant petrol engines, we managed to find a vacant berth amongst the crowd of smartly kept yachts without removing any paint or varnish, or even hitting any of the posts loud enough for anyone in the Club to hear. And later that afternoon the mate arrived with her overnight bag after a fast crossing in the new SS *Arnhem*, bringing an aura of gaiety and the ship's company once more up to strength.

When the mechanic from the Club had examined our silent engine he shook his head and told us what was wrong with the electrical equipment: a new part would have to be obtained, *mijnheer*, but the job would be done properly. With so few days to spare for our cruise it seemed unwise with an engine that might let us down again to continue our plan to take *Lone Gull* through the canals of Amsterdam, and possibly hold up our friends' schedule. We therefore decided to leave the ship where we were while repairs were carried out, and enjoy something of the famed hospitality of this imposing Yacht Club.

The stay also enabled us to see a little of Holland's second city and the ravages brought upon it by the intensive German bombing attacks when the country was being overrun in 1940. We thought our Portsmouth and Plymouth bad enough (we had yet to see Coventry), but it was only too clear that destruction here had been much worse; yet the complete rebuilding of the stricken areas by this admirable and energetic people was in itself a monument to man's indomitable spirit of survival, and it made us think of what these people of Rotterdam must have suffered through the following years of German occupation.

A call to the yachthaven at Huizen where the *Maartje* was lying brought a cheery "No problem. You stay. We come and collect you tomorrow," from Vries. And thus next day we helped our delighted hosts to stack the provisions we had brought into their car, and were at once whisked off on a high-speed sightseeing tour (despite petrol rationing) on our way to the little port in the southern corner of the Ijsselmeer.

– 10 –
Ijsselmeer
by Botter

The *Maartje* proved to be a typical old Zuider Zee fishing botter, built as massively as a church of oak, dark as an old shoe from years of fish oil, and still rigged and in much the same condition as she had been before the owner had brought her out of the fishing trade. From her high curved, ironbound stem to her low pointed stern she was about 12m in length, with a 4m breadth and drawing just about 1m.

The only concessions made to pleasure sailing had been the general fumigation of the fishy hull together with the addition of five berths in the fo'c's'le and primitive form of galley. Alongside the mast, at the end of the long foredeck, a kind of low sentry-box had been fitted which contained the 'heads', a temperamentally wheezy pump toilet. Life on board *Maartje*, we could see, was going to be simple, and quite matey.

From the mast right to the stern she was an open boat with no side decks, but this seemingly immense open space was partly taken up down the centre by a wooden box like an enormous coffin, waist high and about 3m long with removable lids. This was the fish well with free access to the sea in which the catch – mostly eels – could be kept alive. The massive red pine mast, tapered to a point at the truck where the long blue *wimpel* streamed in the breeze, was unstayed except for the iron rod forestay. The short curved gaff and the almost elementary sailing gear were as traditional as the long narrow leeboards and the great rudder.

Rough calculations were to impress us with the thought that this botter's displacement, allowing for the water inside the fish well, would not be less than 19 tonnes, and probably quite a bit more. A lump of a barge, we thought to ourselves, to have to manage in and out of the small harbours of the Ijseelmeer, even though, we noticed, a small box near the tiller hid a very rusty and ancient-looking engine which, Vries told us, had for many years served in a Ford Model T car.

"We do not look at that," he added, closing the lid, "It is not good. We sail."

And sail we did. It was soon clear that Vries had learnt the ways of a fishing botter as a boy, and knew well how to handle this one. The wind was blowing down the narrow entrance of the little harbour, and our skipper proceeded to show us how easy it was to back the old wooden shoe with one of the quant poles out from the berth amongst the rows of very smart yachts until we were clear of the row of white-topped mooring posts, then with helm over to make her swing, set the big foresail and, with a foot or two of leeboard down, head for the entrance.

Hedda, sturdy and muscular, showed me how to set the mainsail with its one halyard, belay it on the single-horned cleat, then hook the downhaul purchase into the massive tack cringle and tweak the luff down until it and the lacing around the mast were truly taut: with the topping lift eased away the heavy mainsail was set nicely without any need to sweat and swig and strain.

"You like to take her, MG," said Vries. "She's all yours."

Thus began a full week's tuition in handling a traditional botter which Fid and I found highly enlightening. We learnt the working of the big foresail (the *botterfok*) with its single sheet long enough for the tail to pass across the mast ready for the next tack, and its short clewline which ran on a traveller along the iron horse across the foredeck, and controlled the flogging of the sail while the botter was in stays, coming round from one tack to the other.

We were to learn how to correct the balance on the helm from fresh breezes to light airs by pushing the 3m long leeboard right down with the boathook whenever, in light breezes, the botter's head started to wander off to leeward, needing some lee helm to keep her on course. Pushing the leeboard down until it was almost vertical gave her the 'bite' in the water she needed and corrected the helm. It was indeed surprising to find how sensitive this heavy old vessel was to the position of her leeboards, and again how nimble she could be in going about in stays or bearing away in a breeze.

Where the old vessel felt heavy was on the helm. After *Lone Gull*, which had been very easy to steer across from Harwich before strong winds, the short tiller of *Maartje* with the big rudder necessary to control all these flat-bottomed craft, seemed just that much harder to control. Steering a botter was no easy tiller-under-the-arm relaxation, but in anything of a breeze it meant braced feet and both arms pulling hard, and at times I longed to rig up tiller lines with, say, a whip purchase to take the strain.

Making short tacks or boards to windward, as with most barges, was hard work. One hand (all right, crew member) was needed to let go the foresheet the moment the sail came aback, and let it crash across the horse; as she came head to wind the other crew member had to jerk the leeboard by its single yoke on to the wale on which the board rested when not in use; then he had to leap smartly to the new lee side to let the other board drop down before the foresail filled on the new tack and the vessel's leeway jammed the leeboard immovable against its wale. Meanwhile the helmsman was leaning hard with his chest against the curved tiller to keep her turning. Sailing a botter or any other sizeable Dutch leeboard craft is no sinecure for the single-hander, however experienced.

Vries and Hedda had promised to show their English friends as many as possible of the small harbours in the Ijsselmeer in the few days we had available, and with indefatigable Dutch energy and enthusiasm they kept their word. We were up at six each morning, breakfasted and under way usually by seven, and Vries counted it only a lazy day's sailing if we did not visit two different ports. Muiden, Monnikendam, Edam in quick succession, then a night at Hoorn with its splendid Brandaris tower at the entrance and its delightful harbour redolent of the days when this was the principal Zuider Zee port for the Dutch East India Company. It is a charming town, and here the goggle-eyed English mariners whispered that they could happily stay at least another night so as to explore the ancient burg. But with wide open eyes Vries would not hear of it.

"But we have many ports yet for you to see," he exclaimed. "Enkhuizen next. It's nicer than Hoorn and only 25 kilometers. Cast off."

He was right, of course. Whilst we foreigners had been captivated by Hoorn and its old buildings we lost our hearts to what we always afterwards thought of as "the town of tinkling bells". For in Enkhuizen the church clocks as well as the town bells not only rang out the hours and the quarters, but every so often added merry tunes that followed before the echoes of the hours had died away. Wherever we strolled through the ancient streets the musical accompaniment seemed to envelop us.

The orderly yacht berths were full of smartly kept craft of both new and traditional types, and Vries was able to point out some of the differing features of the more traditional boats. Here the long shovel bow of a *hoogaarts*, there a *hengst* with a shorter stem but otherwise similar, both from the estuary of the Scheldt, a pair of little round-ended *tjotters*, only half-decked boats with the big fan-shaped leeboards of the inland meers and waterways, while in another part of the harbour he pointed out a *tjalk*, a long apple-bowed steel freighter with a short mast and probably a powerful diesel under the wheelhouse.

Two berths away from us was a fine big white-painted steel *boier* (boo-yer, we learnt to call it) with fan-shaped varnished leeboards and the traditional apple-round bows and matching round stern of this inland water type. There was a jolly party of

local people on board enjoying the sunshine, including a gener-
ously proportioned blonde girl whose singlet and shorts fitted
her as if she had been poured into them and had run over
somewhat in places. As she waved a friendly greeting and
turned to go below Vries whispered with a sly twinkle in his eye
"You see where we Hollanders got our idea for the *boier*'s
stern?"

"It is too bad we have not time," remarked Hedda, giving
him an old-fashioned look, "to go up into Friesland to
Sneekesmeer. It is very pretty, you would like it."

"Or better still," suggested Vries, "go out through the locks
into the Wadde Zee and explore some of our islands like
Vlieland, Terschelling, Ameland, and perhaps a little of our
north coast. We cannot now, but another year, maybe?"

It all sounded very tempting, for even if one did not lock
through the great embankment that dammed the Ijsselmeer off
from the North Sea, this one-time Zuider Zee was ringed with
some thirty or more little ports, all of them charming harbours,
each with its own narrow entrance between jetties, its small
quays guarded by ancient gabled houses, and its own distinc-
tive variety of fishing boat. Vries knew every place from his
youth, and could tell at a glance from which port hailed a
passing *aak*, *klipper* or *tjalk*, a *plutt*, *jol* or *grundel*, a *blazer*, *schokker*
or *zeeuwse schouw*.

He and Hedda tried to get us to remember the significant
differences between vessels coming from the different parts of
the Netherlands, and fell against each other in helpless mirth at
our varied attempts to pronounce some of their Dutch names,
like Gouda, Schouwen, Enkhuizen, Schokland, Terschelling
and Scheveningen. It is indeed tempting to write in more detail
of some of the places we managed to visit, and of the skill with
which Vries worked the *Maartje* in and out of the various
narrow entrances under sail, or using one or other of the
prong-ended quants ("This one for a hard sand bottom, that
one for soft mud"), for he knew them all.

But this is not a guide book, and the old Zuider Zee ports

have been well described elsewhere. Sadly, with the passage of time many of these lovely little harbours have already become a part of the mainland, as the new North East, South East and South West polders have gobbled up the waters of the Ijsselmeer year by year in the great land reclamation scheme. Ere long there will be no expanse of water for sailing on the Ijsselmeer at all, but Holland will be the richer for all this new land.

As we could see from the chart, there were still several other old harbours in the north-east corner of the Ijsselmeer which Vries said he would like to have shown us, such as Hindeloopen, Stavoren ("A great place for the *Stavorse jol,* a comic little boat"), Schokland, Vollenhove and Lemmer and Urk. But time was running short, energetic though our daily sailing was, and for some reason he didn't divulge at the time, as next day was to be Sunday Vries was apparently anxious to press on to make the harbour on the island of Marken, about thirty kilometers away to the south.

For once, as there was hardly a breath of wind, Vries swung the starting handle and, after an asthmatic cough or two, our rusty iron tops'l burst into a spluttering roar. Sedately, as befits a stout old lady, *Maartje* left the musical sound of the bells astern and made her way out of the harbour in a swirl of brown water and a haze of blue smoke.

Outside, in the calm of the morning the huddled rooftops and graceful towers of the little town receded into the distance until the harbour piers could no longer be seen. The land astern and to starboard became a thin straight line, pricked here and there by a pointed church spire, a grotesque water tower, or a tall house with vacant windows.

"Enough of this smelly brute," cried Vries as he turned off the petrol, "before it catches fire, as it often does!"

That, I ruminated, perhaps explained why the inside of the engine case appeared so intensely black. When the engine's racket had died away and *Maartje* gradually lost all her way through the water, a blessed stillness lay over the scene and we found ourselves talking in lowered voices, as though fearful

['With a fair wind across the
Ijsselmeer']

that our voiced thoughts would be carried up to the heavens
and thrown back at us with celestial laughter. It is strange how
the silence of open spaces can make a man feel naked and
vulnerable, as though he was on this earth only by virtue of the
gods' inclination.

As far as the eye could see to the hazy horizon the water lay
like a sheet of glass in the warm sunshine, and the girls gladly
sunbathed on the foredeck. Away to port other Dutch yachts
were moving slowly, the sound of their engines throbbing
across the miles of water in a gentle murmur, while their
reflections writhed gently on the surface.

Accustomed as we English sailors are to our own coastal
tides, Fid and I were captivated by the very stillness of our ship
as she lay becalmed. The shoreline no longer moved past even
perceptibly, and when I took one of the three quants out of its
iron rest along the gunwale, and sounded overside with it, the
pole remained upright in my hands like a fixed beacon post: the
botter was not drifting by an inch.

– 137 –

"At least we're not being set back," was Fid's sleepy comment.

As the day advanced a little breeze crept up from the northwest as Vries had predicted, and *Maartje* came to life. It strengthened by afternoon, causing our old wooden shoe to bustle through the water with gurgles from leeboard and rudder, while we laid our meals out on the handy fishwell top. By mid-afternoon we sailed into the little harbour at Marken, to find it almost jammed with all kinds of fishing craft – botters like *Maartje*, a *hengst* with an Arnemuiden number, a full-bowed *bol* from Stavoren, and a variety of less interesting motor fishing boats, all of them clustered together bows on to the quay.

"All these boats are in port," explained Vries, "because it's Sunday, and they're not allowed to fish on the Lord's Day. But on the stroke of midnight – which is why we've come here – you'll see."

There was one vacant berth between posts amongst some yachts, and we went ashore to explore the little island town. On a Sunday evening it appeared that the local inhabitants by custom paraded up and down the quay in their traditional costumes, showing that Marken had woken up to the attractions of the tourist trade. The men walked past in twos dressed in black velveteen jackets and baggy breeches, cheroots between their lips, while the womenfolk arm in arm tittered by in lace-trimmed black dresses and white bonnets, all of them in *klompen*, the universal wooden sabots of Holland.

Although there were one or two slender girls with winsome faces peering from beneath their tall caps and a pretty enough sight, we had to admit this fake display for the tourists did not appeal to us, nor indeed did Marken itself appear to offer on a Sunday any irresistible diversions. It seemed just a little sad, and we returned to our ship to spend a quiet evening and turn in early.

A few minutes before 12 o'clock our Skipper had Fid and me out into the well, while the two girls decided they were content to stay in their bunks. The strollers had gone from the quay and the harbour lay quiet and still. The moon, nearly full, had risen above the silhouetted rooftops and spires of the town and revealed the mass of masts and rigging of the fishing boats. There was hardly a sound beyond occasional muffled voices from across the water.

The bells of the church tower began their chimes, and struck twelve. It was Monday morning. Almost immediately a diesel engine in one of the boats started its measured *ponk-ponk* beat, followed by another, and more and more until the whole harbour was reverberating with the throb of dozens of engines. Lights had appeared as if by magic on the crowded craft as the whole mass started to move.

As they converged on the narrow entrance between the jetties there came sounds of shock and grinding as the sturdy hulls barged against each other, and the voices of men cheerfully shouting at each other, while the mass of boats jostled through the entrance like sheep driven through a gate.

"We wait until the last has gone," said Vries wisely, "then we go. There is a nice breeze tonight for a good sail."

Once out of the harbour, following closely in the wake of the last stragglers of the fleet we hoisted our mainsail and foresail and began to overhaul first one, then another of the smaller fishing boats, for they were all wallowing along under their engines. Vries had decided to make this a night passage to Harderwijk, one more small port about 22 miles on an east-south-easterly course across this southern corner of the Ijsselmeer. And conditions could not have been better for a quick sail with this quartering wind from the west, and the moon in an almost cloudless sky lighting up the hurrying wavetops.

Indeed, as the land receded out of sight astern, the seas steadily became more boisterous, the fresh water breaking more readily and with more froth than one would expect in the sea – for fresh water has less density ($62\frac{1}{2}$lb for a cubic foot) than seawater (which weights 64lb), and is noticeably more easily fretted by the wind. Wearing both leeboards parked on their wales like a rabbit's ears laid back, *Maartje* was hurrying along with a loud bellow at her bluff bows and a continuous hiss along her sides. Standing in the waist while Fid steered and leaning my arms on the chest-high gunwale, I could imagine this botter was not unlike one of the mediaeval ships carrying troops and their accoutrements on a cross-Channel expedition under a bellying squaresail. Thus would the men spend their time looking over the gunwale across the sea, unless they were miserably seasick. In fact, this way of sailing put me in mind of William the Conqueror's single-masted ships (nefs, I believe) with their side rudders so clearly copied in the Bayeux tapestry, or perhaps three centuries later a square-sterned cogge, also single-masted but now with a stern rudder, on her way to Richard III's great sea victory off Sluys. Just so would these sturdy vessels have run through the night with the helmsman struggling to control them.

This was such a wonderful night to be at sea that I ducked under the mast beam into the forecabin to tempt the girls to come out and share in it. But they were too warm and comfortable to leave their bunks. "If I turn out," said Coppie from under her blankets, "I'm going to be sick. You go and enjoy it." And with a sense of shame I thought of the devotion of all those wives who put up with the privations and discomforts of small boats at sea so as to be with their husbands; and while for the remainder of the night we three men luxuriated in this wonderful moonlit sail, and wished it would even blow harder, the nagging thought remained that all this was not much better than a prolonged ordeal for the girls.

Harderwijk hove in sight over the stemhead as the sun began to rise above the dark line of the coast, and within an hour we were running in between the piers with the mainsail lowered and only the foresail drawing. The faces of the girls reappeared after what they declared had been a beastly and restless night, but after we had tied up in our berth the aroma of bacon, eggs and coffee (and not the ersatz kind still sold in the shops) put a happier atmosphere over all the ship's company.

This was to be our last day with our admirable Dutch

friends, and after a scramble ashore into the town for more provisions, we set sail again before noon and returned to our starting point, in the yachthaven at Huizen, sad to leave Vries and Hedda who had taught us so much about their country and the handling of a real botter.

Lone Gull in the yacht harbour at the Royal Maas was home to us, and after our strenuous days of botter sight-seeing-cruising we were glad of a day's 'stand-easy'. We should have liked to stay a day or two longer to savour the ancient seaport, but Rotterdam was sweltering in a heatwave and the streets were like an oven. Time, too, was pressing and we had to get back.

Coppie was staying with the ship, for as she declared "I'm not going back on the ferry, I'm coming with you. After all, I've got to get used to it *sometime*, waves or no waves!" The Dutch mechanic had done a good job on the engine, which seemed to be working perfectly now, and we decided to start that night at high water, which would be at 2300 hours.

Until the sun had set the thermometer in *Lone Gull*'s cabin stayed at 94 degrees Fahrenheit, and while Fid and I began to single up our lines and prepare the mainsail and staysail for setting towards tide time, we were stripped to the waist and wished there was a breath of wind. It seemed deathly still and sultry in the yacht basin with the moon, just past full, already well up in the sky, and paling the stars with her radiance.

"Are those things little clouds sailing round the moon?" Coppie asked, pointing. "They look just like black witches riding on their broomsticks."

It was indeed a strange sight as we watched several intensely dark clouds with ragged edges race past the face of the moon while we motored out into the broad stream of the river and turned towards the sea. The traffic, never ceasing day or night, was in full swing with its moving lights and rushing bow waves, and the helmsman had to be alert.

We had been motoring for barely half an hour, swept along now on the fierce spring ebb, when the moon became blotted out by a great bank of black cloud. Every now and then the sky was lit up by sheet lightning, and the first puffs of wind from about south-west brought a welcome coolness across the water.

"If this breeze holds, Fid," I said, "we'll get the canvas up, and just about lay it to the Hook."

The words were hardly spoken when the heavens were split by a vivid flash, and with the clap of thunder came a sudden blast of wind that whipped the surface of the river and whistled through the shrouds. There was another blinding flash, another, and yet another while the thunder cracked and boomed above us. Within minutes the wind had risen to a summer gale, tearing at our partly loosened mainsail, and blowing spray from the tops of the wavelets right across our decks.

Some folds of the sail began to flog bwtween their canvas tiers, and while Coppie with her back to the blast held the yacht on course, Fid and I struggled to quieten the mainsail with a more secure stow, and then forward to lash down the restless staysail to the rail. The wind's note in the rigging had risen to a shriek by now and *Lone Gull*, beamy and stiff though she might be, was heeling almost to her rubbing strake under the weight of the wind as Fid and I crawled back to the cockpit to slip hastily into our oilies, while Coppie was advised to stay below out of the stinging wet.

The lightning and the thunder seemed all round us. Vivid flashes, some of them like instant maps of a great river, flicked straight down to the bank to windward with an almost instantaneous crack and boom of thunder. Other flashes spread out more like branches of a tree, lighting up the whole of the sky and the hurrying clouds, while the ensuing thunder roared and rumbled away to the horizon like satanic laughter. So intense and frequent was the lightning that we could scarcely keep our eyes open without being temporarily blinded, and each one of us secretly wondered what would be the effect if our hollow spruce mast was struck.

The engine was put at full throttle to force the ship through the waves as they grew steeper and angrier, and I lowered the centreboard to prevent our being blown bodily across the river to leeward. Indeed for a time we headed straight up to windward to close the invisible weather shore so as to gain better shelter from its high bank. Rain, blown in almost horizontal sheets like stair rods, lashed our faces and for some time between the flashes we could scarcely see where we were heading. We only knew that we were now out of the Old Maas river and were heading down the New Waterway and keeping well over to its western bank.

There was still a great deal of traffic in both directions, bulky ghosts invisible beneath their many lights, and if only to keep well clear of these hurrying monsters we stood well up towards the western side of the channel and out of their way. For the moment the rain had ceased and there seemed to be a short lull in the electric storm, although the wind still continued to shriek and roar in our ears and the spindrift to drive across the ship. Through a break in the clouds racing across the sky the moonlight for a brief moment etched the wildness of the scene: the black surface of the water torn into white foam, a huge deep-laden barge surging past bound up river, and a large coaster passing beyond the barge on her way down to the sea. It was like a black and white photograph flashed for a second or two on the screen.

"What's that light," asked Fid, "off the lee bow?"

For a moment I had assumed it to be the masthead light of another barge, but with a sudden feeling of heartburn I realised it was *stationary*. Just enough light came from the moon to show us then that this light was on an iron beacon, and the truth dawned on me.

"My God, it's a groyne!"

With the tiller slammed hard over, *Lone Gull* began to swing round to starboard, helped with her centreboard down, but as the fierce ebb continued to carry her broadside down it seemed as if she hovered reluctant to keep turning. Not many yards away on our beam we could clearly see the tide rising in a great long mound over the sunken groyne.

Then suddenly with full throttle we were clear of its end and rushing past the light on the iron beacon, and we both began to breathe again. Whether at this state of the tide there would have been just enough water passing over this stone causeway for *Lone Gull* to have ridden over it like a canoe in the rapids, was a useless question; but the thought of what could have been the fate of our ship and her company had my lack of care caused her keel to strike it made us silent in thought for a time. But happily blissful of our narrow escape, Coppie lay on her berth sleeping peacefully.

From then on we carefully picked up one after another of these groynes which reached out from the west bank to the edge of the dredged channel, leaving each beacon well to port. The wind was gradually veering more to the westward, yet howling as loudly as ever, while the spray began to feel colder every minute. The heat of the evening had been all blown away. We were not far now from the Hook, for *Lone Gull* was beginning to sense a swell that was rolling in from the entrance, a warning of what the seas must be like with this outpouring tide meeting the onshore gale.

It was no time to try to go out and set course westerly for Harwich, and we decided to bring up between two of the groynes and wait for low water and less wind. As we headed inshore the leadline showed no bottom at 12 metres, until we were well within the line between two of the beacons, when the lead suddenly hit the ground at two metres. The edge of the channel must have been dredged as steep as the side of a house, and we let go in the shallow water and stopped the engine.

At least this respite gave us an opportunity to dry off and calm down with a mug of cocoa all round. But with this swell running in it was a very restless berth, and we knew that if we stopped here too long we should take the ground. Dawn was breaking, however, and it would soon be light enough for us to up anchor and go and find the entrance to the Berghaven, the little harbour shown on the chart on the other side of the

Waterway behind the packet boat quays at the Hook, where we hoped there would be shelter and a quiet berth.

Some two hours later we steamed in between the piers and gratefully accepted a berth for the time being alongside a smart Dutch naval tug, whose captain and crew could not have been more helpful. And while we had breakfast the wild wind of the night with its black clouds passed away, and as the sun rose into a clear sky the wind died altogether. The heatwave was upon us once more.

"Very bad storm last night, ja?" Our friends leant along the tug's rail and grinned. "But our forecast say fine weather, much sun, little wind. Gut for sail to England, ja?"

Our fuel tank was more than half empty and they obligingly helped us fill it with the last of our petrol coupons. They also had orders to get underway at 1100 hrs, and gave us a tow alongside before casting us off in midstream with many waves and our grateful thanks. We were on our way again.

Until late in the afternoon the North Sea was like a mirror in the haze, and smoke from the tall chimneys on shore rose into the sky in straight columns. Ships following the swept channels along the coast appeared to stand high out of the water, with long writhing reflections reaching towards us. *Lone Gull's* engine purred steadily as we made a brisk 5½ knots on our course for the Naze, but at last, as evening advanced, a gentle breeze from south-east crept across the water, the engine was switched off, and our sails were set and drawing nicely with the white ghoster tautening its single sheet.

All night the breeze stayed fair while our little ship rustled quietly over the smooth sea, and Coppie took her regular watches at the helm while Fid and I turned in. With daylight the Sunk light vessel rose above the horizon like a splash of red, and soon the group of erections known as the Roughs Tower (so recently manned as an ack-ack platform, and in a few years to be adopted as the Kingdom of Sealand) came up over the edge of the sea like crouching monsters.

The low cliffs of the Naze spread themselves slowly across

the horizon and beyond our bowsprit the two-hundred-year-old seamark, the Naze Tower, greeted us like an old friend. With the young flood tide making by now the Wallet seemed to receive us with joy, for we were once again in our own home waters. And in a few hours Fid's own *Ben Gunn* would be there, waiting for us on her nearby mooring in the Besom Fleet.

[The Waterfront, Maldon]

– 11 –

A cross on
the Gunfleet

As we stood out from the Ray Gut close-hauled to a light easterly breeze, the boats brought up off Southend pier had already turned to the ebb.

"Well, we haven't lost much of our tide," said my Skipper as his pipe crackled in sympathy, "but if we're to make the Orwell today we'll darn well need every minute of it with this light breeze."

The horizon beyond the Estuary was clear like a blue-grey pencil line against the midday sky, with hardly a white flash here and there to show where the gentle wind was able to tumble a little wave crest over against the young ebb. Almost hull down beyond the low point of Shoeburyness, the brown sails of two barges were etched against the sky as they worked their way slowly, tack by tack with the wind a little north of east, down Swin.

This was not the first time I had crewed for Barney aboard his little white barge yacht, *Curlew*, in these self-same waters (see *Swatchways and Little Ships*) but this time we had company on board with us. Spritty and Meow between them were to keep us constantly amused on this mini-cruise. Fully expecting that we were going to sail for some time, Meow's marmalade-coloured body was curled up in his usual choice of resting place, on the Skipper's bunk in the cabin, his striped tail wrapped half round him. With his broad head and wise brown eyes he was a handsome animal (and knew it), the kind of cat you would normally find lording it over the other creatures in some stables – except that, as Barney would say, he was only half a tom, having, as it were, been defused.

The summer's afternoon wore on as *Curlew* made short tacks between the Maplin sands and the edge of the West Barrow, following faithfully in the wake of the two spritties which were steadily gaining on us ahead. *Curlew* was a 30ft Tredwen barge with iron leeboards, rigged as a gaff sloop with a roller fores'l at the stemhead, and she slopped and waddled lazily over the short little seas ruffled by the head wind, in the purposeful way small barges always seem to enjoy – a long way in a long time.

"Spritty, come aft, you idiot," said Barney. "You'll only fall overboard again."

The dog continued to stand by the roller of the fores'l for a few moments longer, before reluctantly turning and padding gingerly aft along the barge's narrow weather deck. He was no thoroughbred, but with his black and white rough coat, floppy ears, melting brown eyes and big, almost clumsy, paws an admirer *could* claim that he looked like some sort of springer spaniel.

"He'd stand all day looking down over the bows, if I let him," Barney added with a grin as Spritty settled on the after deck beside his master at the tiller. "If it's choppy he champs at every bit of spray that comes aboard, but he's already fallen overboard once, and he wasn't all that easy to haul back aboard again, were you, old man?" The spaniel responded with a rapid thumping of his tail on the deck.

"What does Meow think of life aboard?"

"Oh him, he's quite at home," my friend laughed. "Always discovers the warmest and driest spot, never seasick like old Spritty has been once or twice, and knows very well just where I keep the condensed milk and the tins of sardines."

"A really sage animal, in fact?"

"Well, cats as a rule are much better than dogs at looking

after themselves – they're like old soldiers. A good dog, like this rascal here, is a faithful, dependent companion and seems to need his master's presence, and his affection for him. A cat, like that ginger semi-tom pretending to be fast asleep on my bunk, on the other hand is completely independent and self-sufficient. If he's not in the mood to be nursed and stroked, he'll flick his tail and stalk away for'ard. But," Barney paused to light his pipe behind cupped hands, "in their different ways they're marvellous companions to have on board. You'll see."

The sun was getting low over the distant Essex shore as the round shape of the Swin Spitway cage buoy sidled lazily past, the clappers striking the deep toned bell only intermittently in the gentle swell. *Curlew* nosed her way through the shallow channel between the sands into the waters of the Wallet, and began to fetch close-hauled towards the distant Naze. The breeze, never strong during the day, seemed to be slowly dying with the sun, and progress over the ground as the ebb finished its course, and the first trickle of the flood tide turned against us, became less and less.

Barney sniffed with the wind coming across the miles of bare Gunfleet sands to seaward of us, bringing with it scents of wet seaweed and salt pools, the exciting tang of the sea, and glanced round at the evening sky.

"No point in plugging on against a foul tide," he said. "Let her come round, and we'll stand in to the edge of the sands on this tack and find a snug berth for the night. I think I know the place."

Curlew quietly obeyed, and as we steadily sailed away from the coast on the port tack I could make out ahead the golden line of the dried-out sands between us and the sea. Some two miles distant through the weather rigging the gaunt red pile of the Gunfleet lighthouse stood astride on its legs guarding the other edge of the sands in the King's Channel.

"There's a shallow inset like a tiny bay in the sands here-abouts," Barney was saying, "and if my cross bearings of the lighthouse and that can buoy there (that's the Wallet No 4) are spot-on, we should be able to find it for the night. Spritty knows it well," he added as the tail thumped happily again on the deck. "I've often given him a run ashore here, when bound through the Wallet."

I also had more than once brought up for a foul tide along the edge of these sands in my own boats, when the wind was coming in from the sea anywhere between east and south-west, and found as quiet shelter while the sands to windward were uncovered as one could expect in any river anchorage. I was interested to see therefore what Barney called his special anchorage.

With the sounding lead we edged in towards the line of sand until the depth was less than five feet.

"It's only just gone low water," said my Skipper quietly, "and that'll be plenty for our two-foot draught. This'll do nicely, don't you think?"

While he went forward to let go the hook. I rolled up the foresail with its line in the cockpit, and then lowered the gaff. Spritty was on the side deck his black nose quivering with the scents to windward, his stumpy tail wagging like a vibrator. And looking around I could make out the thin curve of sand stretching out to each side of us, almost enclosing us in a little bay with a steep edge that rose perhaps a foot above the water. Provided the wind didn't breeze up during the night from the north or west – and from experience I knew we should both be awake on the instant – Barney really had found a lovely little sheltered anchorage.

"It was only last year that I discovered this bay," he said modestly. "In fact it might have only been formed with the previous gales, and by next year it might well disappear altogether, for as you know the run of these sands alters with every winter's bad weather."

Spritty was whining every now and then, impatient to go ashore. Barney laughed.

"While I get supper ready," he said, "will you mind taking the animal for a run ashore and get him to empty himself for the night? He must want to by now."

"What about Meow?" I queried. "Hold him over the side?"

"No need. He's got his own sand box in the fo'c's'le. He's well trained."

The spaniel blundered into the dinghy almost before I had the little pram alongside, and while I rowed the few yards to the edge of the sand he stood in the bows sniffing the air, with his paws on the forward transom and his tail little more than a furry blur. In fact, he was over the bow and splashing in the shallow water before the pram grounded.

Some distance away a flock of redshank with some dunlin stalked the tideline on tiny mincing feet. With excited yelps Spritty dashed after them, leaping up and down through the shallow water, his ears flapping in time with his barks. The birds waited until he was within a few yards of them, then rose in a small cloud. With a sweeping gesture of defiance they settled again at the water's edge a hundred yards farther on.

Undismayed, Spritty continued to leap and splash in the direction of the waders, while a gull separated itself from its companions in the sky and swooped down over the dog in a flash of white and black. Spritty merely became more frenzied as his quarry took off again when only yards away, while his barking became fainter and fainter in the distance. Seated on the dinghy's gunwale I began to wonder how long he and the birds would keep this caper going, and whether they would lure the brainless idiot as far as the Spitway before he gave up trying to fly. At least, this was quite the most sedentary way of exercising a dog that I had come across, and had I been a smoker I should probably have lit a pipe and waited in comfort, chuckling at the animal's absurd antics.

There was no need to worry about losing him, however, for between them the waders and the gulls took it in turns to alight on the sand and then take off all round him, teasing him with their piping cries, until he came loping back to the dinghy with lolling tongue and a face grinning with contentment. And when at last he recalled the principal reason why I had brought him ashore, and showed his contempt for those tantalising birds, he dutifully leapt back into the pram, and took up his stance with paws on the bow transom once more.

It might have been the tempting aroma of Barney's cooking or over eagerness to get home, but as I brought the pram up to the barge's stern Spritty took a flying leap, almost stopping the dinghy in its tracks, missed his footing at the rail, and fell into the water with a heavy splash. His owner's head popped up through the hatch.

"That silly animal gone overboard again?" he grinned. "Come up, you wet rascal," and between us we yanked the spaniel like a sodden hearthrug on to the deck. And while I made the painter fast with my face at deck level what must Spritty do but give himself a good shake like a lawn sprinkler, and half drench me.

"Oh, you wet horror," was all I could mutter, while for good measure he leant over and gave my face a boisterous lick in over-affectionate greeting. Nature, I couldn't help thinking, could have no sense of proportion in supplying so friendly an animal with such a long tongue, but I couldn't resist giving his squirming flank a friendly hug.

It was after we had finished supper and were yarning in the cockpit in the last rays of the sunset that Meow condescended to come stalking out of deck, surveyed the scene with a proprietary air, and with an audible purring rubbed his broad head against us in turn. The humans in the party felt strangely honoured, wearing the kind of expressions they do when asked to admire a friend's new baby. Then the dog and cat began their evening capers.

Meow scampered along the deck with Spritty after him, ears flapping like wings, then with consummate grace the cat sprang up on to the gaff jaws and crouched, tail twitching, ears laid down, eyes giving the dog beneath him the stare of an angry tiger. Spritty jumped and barked in vain; Meow's paw merely struck at the dog's wet nose whenever it came within reach. Then with a supercilious sneer on his face the cat stood

['The fish jumping plagued Meow']

up, tail erect, and proceeded in an unhurried mincing walk to come aft along the gaff, insinuating himself past the peak halyard wire span with liquid ease, while his would-be tormentor leapt along the starboard side deck with threatening yelps.

. At the peak end of the gaff, just over our heads, Meow paused to regard the dog below him while his own tail twitched provocatively, then jumped softly down onto the cabin top, ran forward again and sprang up the mast almost in one movement. From here he dropped back on to the stowed mainsail and once more led the spaniel a dance, back and forth with twitching tail, just out of reach.

This game of catch-us-catch-can went on for several minutes while Barney and I held our sides at the animals' antics.

"Spritty got his own back once," said Barney as he refilled his trusty pipe. "One still evening we were lying in the Stour, and the fish started jumping. There seemed to be scores of them, grey mullet I expect, all round us. Meow was crouching over the bow with his whole body twitching with excitement, watching them, and then I saw Spritty move very quietly up to the foredeck with his body dropped low, like a shepherd's dog guarding sheep. He moved cautiously up to where the cat was crouching, put his muzzle under Meow's hindquarters and – wallop! Meow was overboard and Spritty barking with delight. And a pretty bedraggled thing the cat looked when I fished him out. Yet they're the best of pals really."

The two quadrupeds continued to give us unlimited amusement with their feints and gambols until they both tired and it was time to turn in. Their berth was on a blanket on one of the two pipecots in the fo'c's'le, and before blowing out the cabin lamp I peered in to look at them. Spritty was flaked out on his side with his great paws stretched out beyond the edge of the cot, while Meow was curled up between them, his head resting against his pal's leg and a smile that I could only describe as wider than his own face: a picture of nursery bliss. Even then Spritty's tail shook a little and one eye half-opened when he sensed that they were being looked at.

"Good night, little friends," I whispered, "Sleep well."

Two days later, after we had sailed into Walton Backwaters and up the Stour to Mistley and back, I reluctantly left the ship at Pin Mill to return to London and the office desk. But of the three happy days I had spent aboard the *Curlew* the most engaging memories were those of the playful fights and endearing ways of the two pets.

Barney made Pin Mill his base for the rest of that season, where the sight of his little barge yacht with a black and white spaniel usually on the foredeck was a familiar sight to other sailors on the lovely Orwell. I was keeping my own boat *Nightfall* at Heybridge at that time, and as most weekends when I could get away were spent sailing around the Blackwater,

Colne and Crouch waters, I did not run across my friend's ménage.

In fact, it must have been nearly two years after our little cruise together that I next sighted the *Curlew* at anchor. Once more single-handed, I was working *Nightfall* up from the Pye End buoy into the Walton Channel with a light westerly just as the first of the ebb started to run down against us. At the mouth of the creek leading up to Foundry Hard I let go, and while stowing the sails noticed my friend's little barge lying on her anchor a little farther up the Twizzle.

Barney wasn't looking his usual rubicund self when I rowed alongside and greeted him.

"Fact is," he said, "I've just lost old Spritty."

He must have seen the look on my face, for he turned away.

"The vet here in Walton couldn't do anything for him," he added. "Said his heart had just given out. The little old chap, you see, was getting on – nearly twelve, a fair age for a spaniel. The vet wrapped his body up for me so I could bring him back on board this morning. Now I'm afraid I've got a sad duty to perform," and he looked out past the high ground of the Naze where the tower stood above the skyline.

"A proper sea burial?"

Barney nodded. "Something like that, Somewhere I know he'd love to be. I suppose you wouldn't care to . . . ?"

Of course. I joined my old friend aboard after we had left my own dinghy fast to *Nighfall*'s stern. The westerly breeze, although not more than a force three, was still holding steadily and *Curlew* bustled happily down on the ebb to the Pye End, where we gybed her and headed for the Naze. I suspect she knew where she was going.

No need to ask about Meow. The cat was curled up asleep on the skipper's berth in his usual place, purring a little when I stroked him.

"He seemed puzzled at first," said Barney. "Couldn't make it out. But like a cat he's accepted the unexplainable and just made himself comfortable. Sometimes I wish I was a cat."

Curlew made steadily over the ebb as she brought Walton pier on the beam and we hauled our sheets for a close fetch across the Wallet with the Gunfleet lighthouse fine on the lee bow. The sands were uncovering and showed almost golden against the horizon in the afternoon sun. My Skipper was on the foredeck studying the lie of the shoals through his binoculars.

"That's the place," he indicated, pointing ahead. "I can just make out the end of the little bay showing against the shallows."

A few minutes later the hook was let go and the sails stowed in much the same position, as far as I could recall, as we had anchored in two years before. The yacht lay quietly with the edge of the sands lying in a gentle curve half-way round her, a secret little bay.

"You'll think me a sentimental old fool," Barney was saying, "but I made this in Bedwell's old boat shed in Mill Lane this morning." It was a simple little wooden cross about two feet long, nicely made and pointed at the base, and with the name 'Spritty' in small letters punched with a sharp spike into the crosspiece.

Over on the sands I took the spade we had brought with us and dug a hole, surprised how heavy and tenacious the sand was to prise apart. Then we lowered the pathetic little bundle into the grave and covered it over. The cross we hammered into the sand nearby.

As we got underway again for the Twizzle we had a last look at the solitary cross looking tiny and forlorn amidst the stretch of yellow sand.

"The old *Curlew*," said Barney quietly, "will never be quite the same again, even with Meow aboard."

A few weeks later I was sailing past the spot with three friends aboard *Nightfall*, having come down from Heybridge on the ebb, and searched the tideline with the glasses. And there it was, a tiny cross near the edge of the sand. I said nothing to my pals, for they didn't know Barney nor Spritty, and it could not be long before easterly gales and the tides would bury it, and probably within a year or two the bay itself would disappear as the sands changed their contours. But I have often wondered if any passing barge skipper or sailing man ever noticed the solitary little mark on the sands before it went altogether.